Pangyrus

For information about permission to reproduce selections from this book,
please write to Permissions at info@pangyrus.com

The text of this book is set in Palatino
with display text set in Crimson and Baskerville
Composition by Yahya Chaudhry and Abraar Chaudhry
Cover design by Douglas Woodhouse

Editor: Greg Harris
Managing Editor: Jess McCann
Associate Managing Editor: Robin Beaudoin
Managing Editor, Print Edition: Ahna Wayne Aposhian
Fiction Editors: Anne Bernays, Sarah Colwill-Brown
Poetry Editor: Cheryl Clark Vermeulen
Nonfiction Editor: Marie Danziger
Comics Editor: Dan Mazur
Contributing Editors: Kalpana Jain, Carmen Nobel
Reviews Editor: Chris Hartman
Social Media Assistant: Yahya Chaudhry
Newsletter Editor and Marketing Assistant: Graeme Harcourt
Graphic & Web Designers: Esther Weeks, Dolphia Nandi
Copy Editors: Chris Hartman,
Ahna Wayne Aposhian, Rachel Zwiebel
Business Manager: Lakeisha Landrum
Logo Design: Ted Ollier

Pangyrus
79 JFK Street, L103
Cambridge, MA 02138
pangyrus.com

Contents

Pangyrus

Note from the Editor

No one knows, showing up on the shores of a strange country, clutching an address on an envelope, where the journey will lead. "I have something important to tell you from your family in Polish Szrensk," my great-grandmother reportedly said to my great-grandfather, the first time they met as adults in Columbus, Georgia. She spoke not a lick of English; she never learned to read. She was a teenager who'd been in the U.S. maybe a few weeks. "They've found a wife for you."

"Tell them it's too late," he said, covering her hand with his. "I've just found one on my own."

When you're as poor as my great-grandparents were when they made their way to the U.S. from eastern Europe, immigration means risk. A branch of the family went dark, as a father parked his children in an orphanage and disappeared somewhere in Texas. Another branch staggered under tragedy and suicide, when a husband couldn't provide, and a wife, abandoned to raise five children on the meager proceeds of a millinery shop in Washington, D.C., crumbled.

Immigration also means adapting. The son of an old-world scholar got staked some home goods, and learned to run a store in Alabama. A cousin became one of the first women doctors in California. Two generations of engineers arose, military specialists who helped hone radar technology in World War II, and nuclear submarines in the Cold War.

The submariner was my father, and when he came through the door after a thirteen-month deployment to Scotland, I didn't recognize the red-bearded, uniformed man who handed me the die-cast double-deck-er bus toy. At that point, our American identity was so thick I habitually stood and put my hand on my chest when the TV played the national anthem. It never even occurred to me, until I was older and became curious about family history, that we had been, or could be, anything else. Growing up in 13 different houses in 7 different states, I played with friends whose parents and grandparents had immigrated from Japan and Russia and the Philippines and Guam and Czechoslovakia, all of us as American as anyone else.

Roman Jakobson, the towering Russian language theorist who originated, with Saussure, structural linguistics, and with others, modern phonology and semiotics—had as his fundamental observation that distinctions require difference. We make a sound with our tongue pressed against the roof of our mouth in one way, and it's a 't'. Press a little more, and it's a 'd'. Tip-toe to the teeth, and it's 'th'. Each sound is what it is, because it is not the other, and someone equipped with the code—who speaks English, and hears the variations—will interpret them accurately.

America stands out because its distinction is not primarily differences among Americans—there isn't a "real" American ethnicity—but differences with 'the old country'. All the 'old countries' where our ancestors came from, even those displaced unwillingly, or from native life on this continent. America is a place where all stories connect, a place of democracy, of citizenship through law. There are words, all of them associated with revulsion, for Americans who try to draw distinctions among Americans: Bigotry. Prejudice. Bias. Hate.

And because distinction requires difference, and because *Pangyrus* as a project was born, in one stretched telling, when as a 7th-grader in Hawaii I dreamed of becoming a writer, it's worth revisiting what makes it, in all its international curiosity, and broad fascination with cultural and literary forms, an American journal. And it is simply this: some Wednesday that year, the teachers at my Hebrew school ushered us from beneath the plumeria trees and off the basketball courts to sit in a dark classroom, where flickering movies played against the wall. In them the gaunt skeletons of the old country staggered in lines to be shorn of hair, consumed in fire, and laid as piles of shattered bones in the ashes of the Holocaust.

Those were the people my great-grandparents might have been—before they became laughing, funny round storytellers of the Ballyhoos, the dances where they socialized from New Orleans to Atlanta. Those skeletons were us—and not-us. There was a difference. A distinction. We had grown up in safety. We had grown up with a belonging that no one in the old country ever would know.

Roman Jakobson, too. He was a contemporary of my great-grandparents. He fled the Nazis, walking on foot at one point out of Norway as it went over to the fascists. He ended up a professor at Harvard and MIT. We might have seen each other on campus, fellow Americans; he an 89-year-old emeritus, me a one-year-old in my father's arms, some afternoon when he took a break from his studies in naval architecture.

This journal, this labor of love of so many people, is outreach. It is record. It is dedicated to people in all parts of the world, in the spirit of a place where all may connect, where imagination and empathy and knowledge and art do their utmost to find the human in us humans.

—Greg Harris

Invincible

by Maggie Smith

The babies made me invincible.
Even as they slept, they protected me.
Even as they slept, I could stomach the dark.
I could walk up the stairs, lights out,
and pass the mirror without hurrying.
I was divine, hovering inches above the floor
in a cloud sweet as milk—no rose perfume
like Therese. I glowed with love but also
with suffering. Even the suffering
I wore like a blue robe, beautiful enough
for a painting. I felt the sky guarding me.
When I wore the babies and under
the babies the blue robe of my suffering,
I was lit from within. I burned myself
for fuel, shoveling black stones into
the stove inside me. The milk boiled
and grew skin. It turned. Still I felt nothing
could harm me—nothing would dare.
I was essential. I was too needed
in the world. That feeling was a spell
that is only now beginning to break.

Fern Gully

by Jonathan Escoffery

*I*f, on a first and final return to your parents' island as a unit, your family must choose between routes to Jamaica's northern coast from Kingston, know this: Both twist over cliffs, at inclines that compel drivers to build velocity and zoom blindly around bends. Both force cars to hug brink or escarpment when dodging oncoming traffic. But—assuming your family survives this drive—only one of these routes will take you through Fern Gully.

Fern Gully is supernatural. It's tunnel grown of ferns; pulsating walls, curved up into a chlorophyllous canopy. It's acid green, searing through your eyes into your brain.

If your parents take this route, make sure they pull off the thoroughfare and exit the car with you. Let your mom hold your hand, but when she's not paying attention break away into a field of lime-green fiddleheads grown taller than you'll ever be. Their fibers dangle white, as thick as your hair. Try to wrap your hands around one's stalk. Grasp its felt-like fibers, downy and supple on your palm. This is softer than anything you will feel again. Kneel to inspect a newborn fern, one that's sprung to your knee. Rub your finger along the curve of its head. Feel the frond's silky baby fleece.

If your mother calls after you, if she says it's time to leave, pluck this fiddlehead from the earth, and keep it as proof of magic. If you wait to ask permission, she will tell you not to bother. "We have ferns in our backyard," she will say.

You'll ask why you've never seen them. How could you have never noticed? She'll promise to point them out when you get back.

When you return to the States—not the first day, but after she has rested some—she will take you out back, and point to a plant in a white pot sitting on the ground, and say, "See? See?"

And you will see nothing, nothing but a dull green houseplant.

Will You Line Up the Children?

by Carrie Oeding

For pigtails, balance beams, cracks to break your mother's back.
Everything, lines.

I wrote loops, not over and over but forward and forward and
my line was a graphite bow, a graphite flight performing an air
show, a telephone cord to stories and signatures, a sideways gallop.

Put a word in. Even *bird*. Not even a kind of bird.
I would write that bird to be a lace bird a paltry bird a saffron
sparkle word bird.

That year all the words would fall into my lines.

Even *chair* for you to sit down while my line kept going.
I would learn cursive and go.
I was a dot in Minnesota on I-90.
I had learned about the west and the east.

A ray is a dot with a line leaving it that never ends.

This young thing wants to pirouette on the power lines.
This young thing says his thoughts are kite string.

I am putting children in all of my lines—

I have a tightrope to skim above the sea.
An assembly line of square cheese.
Language meet lines. Lines meet language.
Those Cy Twombly chalk squiggles. Knots of excuses.
Flaneur through garbage. A stomp to the bus.

Children, fall into me. Make breasts, silhouettes.
I've been writing lines all of this time.

Detectives

by Julie Wittes Schlack

I'm not sure why I chose Howie Herskovisy to be my partner in solving mysteries. Perhaps it was because, a year younger than me and living one very long block away, he dwelled outside my everyday social circles. Or perhaps, in his freckled blondness and quiet dreaminess, I recognized both the exotic and the familiar.

Our first case involved Mrs. Alter, the woman my parents had hired to come to our house two afternoons a week to cook and clean while they were at work. She was a broad, lumbering Polish woman in her early fifties, with wide shoulders and thick ankles that ballooned out of the tops of the black-laced boots that she wore on even the hottest of summer days. A thin layer of greasy perspiration coating the broken blood vessels in her nose and cheeks gave her clenched face a red and glistening veneer. Her light-blue eyes were locked in a perpetual squint, and when the sun streaming into the house struck the wire frames of her glasses, they seemed to emit predatory daggers of light. Swollen and sagging, the bosom that strained against her flowered dress created the impression of someone both inflated and defeated at the same time. Or, as I thought then, mean.

Beyond the fact that she spoke very little English, Mrs. Alter was profoundly foreign, smelling sourly of cabbage and sweat, and always grumpy. She'd scrub the counters with a frightening vigor, as if expecting to uncover gold dust beneath the robin's-egg Formica. Then she'd take a break and sit down at one end of the narrow kitchen table, a glass of hot tea in front of her, with a tablespoon resting in it, she explained, to "eat the heat." Pressing a sugar cube to her front teeth with her tongue, she'd take frequent, short sips, imbibing in loud, hissing bursts that reminded me of a snake I'd seen on a TV show, inhaling a live mouse.

My brother and I complained about her to our parents. Why did we need her? How come she smelled so bad? Why did she only make stupid hard cookies with poppy seeds instead of soft ones that oozed with melting chocolate chips?

"Don't be mean just because she's different," my mother would chastise us. "Mrs. Alter doesn't have an easy life."

That brought our complaining to a dead stop. We were supposed to feel bad for people who didn't have easy lives. We were to treat them with kindness and respect, and help them if we could. But what was so hard about her life?

"Her son's a no-goodnick," my mother said to my father over dinner one night, "and her daughter-in-law's even worse. It's not like they're hurting for money. Who puts their mother out to work cleaning other peoples' houses if they don't have to? It's not just unkind. There's something, I don't know, unseemly about it."

"Unseemly" sounded criminal to me. If Mrs. Alter's son and daughter-in-law were mean to her, surely they were up to other nefarious activities as well.

Our love of detective stories wasn't unique to Howie and me. Children are still drawn to Nancy Drew and The Hardy Boys, to Encyclopedia Brown and Timmy Failure. These characters have physical courage but also smarts. They're spunky, with a sense of their own agency that all kids aspire to and lucky ones have. But there's more to it than that. Adult interactions are encrypted. Grownups use code words for sentiments that are too impolite to explicitly express, small gestures like shrugs and eye rolls to convey who is to be pitied, scorned, or simply ignored. They borrow phrases from other languages, exchange long and opaque gazes when someone has transgressed by being too noisy or too quiet, too demonstrative or too restrained, too smart or too stupid. Kids understand that to grow up, they must first decipher, then adopt the code. So they learn to love looking for clues. They seek triumph in the face of the dangers they have invented.

Howie and I started, as all good detectives do, with footprints. In 1963, Cote St. Luc was a neighborhood expanding into a suburb as it strained ever westward, and even the four-block walk from Westminster School to my house revealed its striations. The two-block area surrounding the school comprised bungalows and small ranch houses built immediately post-war. When we moved into our split-level ranch house in 1956, we were its first occupants, and Howie's family was the first to inhabit their semi-detached townhouse. But just a couple of blocks south and west of mine, new roads and large brick homes – free standing and almost palatial with their arched doorways, multiple floors, and garages that opened and closed with the push of a button – were being built in what had been empty fields.

And in front of them were freshly poured sidewalks, rich with clues. Despite being cordoned off by thick red string, the rectangles of wet concrete held imprints and etchings. Howie and I tried to decode them as we patrolled the new streets, looking for footprints. Some, my father had told me – the ones with neatly stenciled arrows and letters like *SW* or *30V* – indicated where water lines and electrical cables met in submerged junctions. Others – the messy scrawled initials, five- and six-pointed stars, and the hand-prints – were clearly made by other kids.

We ignored the handprints, and after only a couple of forays, found signs of steps. But they were never more than one or two consecutive footprints, traces that trailed off like an unfinished thought.

"They must be trying to escape detection," I told Howie. Still, we stayed on the trail, scouting the newly named Wolseley Avenue, speculating as to why the evil daughter-in-law and weak-willed son wanted Mrs. Alter out of the house. It might have been so that they had time and space in which to sort their stolen jewels, or so that they could counterfeit their money in peace. Or perhaps, given the proximity of the train yard, they were smugglers.

Besides being the possible site of the Alter family iniquity, the train yard held another fascination. With its lack of houses and people, its expanse of nothing but track, dirt, and a handful of mute, permanently-parked freight cars, it was the most likely site in Cote St. Luc for quicksand. I knew all about quicksand, having seen not just the *Lassie* episode in which Timmy gets stuck in it, but also the "Sky King" episode in which, thanks to some mighty fine piloting by Sky King, Penny is able to toss a lasso down from the low-flying, circling Cessna to the robber who is sinking fast below them. As the viscous sand laps him in, the robber faces a choice: throw away the satchel of loot that he's stolen from the bank in order to grab hold of the lifesaving rope that will lift him to safety, or be swallowed alive, a victim of his own greed. For that was the nature of quicksand – it didn't distinguish between the good, like Timmy, and the bad, like that stupid robber, and it was indistinguishable from solid ground.

We went to the train yard prepared. I wore my red pedal-pushers so that I wouldn't get any quicksand on the cuffs of my pants, and though I had no lasso, I did bring my yo-yo. As usual,

Howie was sitting outside on the front stairs to his house, and silently joined me as I parked my bike in front of my aunt and uncle's. We had walked to the dead end of Westluke before, but this was the first time that we'd ever actually stepped over the rounded curb and onto the hard-packed dirt, studded with bottle caps and rounded bits of glass. As we neared the tracks, we turned left and, eyes to the ground, paced slowly in parallel to them. But if there were footprints, we couldn't discern them in the mottled mix of hardened mud and tufted weeds. The rusty CNR freight cars had no hobos sleeping in them, nor were there small bands of white slaves or fugitive Nazis cowering beneath them. Even now I'd like to say that there were bills of counterfeit money blowing forlornly in the late-afternoon breeze, or that we'd found the papery skeleton of a rabbit or a lost cat. But we saw little besides rocks and puddles, and the naked sides of the last houses on each block.

It was nearing dusk, and the blue-grey sky was made darker by rain clouds blowing in. Thunder growled nearby, and as we headed back, first jogging, then in a flat-out dash, the skies opened up and we were blasted by rain. The already-damp ground turned instantly slick and I slid, falling flat on my chest. Howie helped me up; we kept running. The hard-packed dirt loosened under the pounding, turning into a sticky, oozing mud, and a minute later, one of my canvas sneakers got stuck in the muck and my foot lifted right out of it. I stopped for a second to try to retrieve it, but Howie kept going, and I was afraid to stand still, panicked that the ground would grasp more than my shoe.

I was covered in mud by the time I got back to my bike. Howie was already in his house. He'd left me alone on the abandoned block. When I got home, my mother made me strip off my dripping clothes in the foyer, despite the fact that Jerry Marcus was there playing floor hockey with my brother. She wrapped me in a bath towel, and as she marched me through the house to the tub, Jerry, the friend of my brother who I most despised, poked his head out from the top of the basement stairs and, in his best Woody Woodpecker voice, cawed *Uh uh uh AW uh*. My humiliation was complete.

That was probably the last of my adventures with Howie. Years later I heard that he'd become a dentist, and that his mother left his father for a failed affair with Sheila Fineberg's father down the block. I can no longer hear his voice, let alone anything he may have said. I remember his fair complexion and his placidity, which I didn't recognize as sadness. He was my uncritical companion on those still afternoons when we strayed from the familiar onto brand-new blocks, where nobody was known, nobody knew us, and everything but the inscrutable faces of the houses themselves was imagined.

Were we just like any suburban kids, living at any time in any place? Or were we attuned to the zeitgeist, sensing if not knowing that 1962 held some very real, very big secrets.

Three years earlier, the United States' satellite program had been launched, not to promote communication, but surveillance. An orbiting Corona satellite would shoot photographs of secret facilities around the world, then jettison the film canisters. Fifty thousand feet over the Pacific, as the canisters delicately drifted downward – their flight slowed by a brightly colored parachute – a crew of ten skilled pilots, lassoers, and winch operators would snatch the film capsules out of mid-air and reel them in to their aircraft. After landing, they'd place the film on another aircraft that would transport it to Maryland for analysis. This process, making it possible to see what was going on around the globe in an operation that required mere days to complete, demanded an extraordinary meld of engineering, logistics, and human skill. But of course, it wasn't publicized, let alone celebrated.

During the 1962 Cuban Missile Crisis, provoked by satellite

images of Soviet missiles ensconced in Cuba, there had certainly been nothing festive about our family's abrupt mid-week excursion to the country house in St. Adolphe. Secretly warned by the head of the Canadian military – brother of a Canadian Air Force friend of my Uncle Herbie's – that nuclear war was imminent and we should get out of Montreal, our parents loaded up the cars with my cousins, my brother, and me, and cases of canned goods and fled the city. Though the five of us kids often played soldier, marching in lockstep while chanting "Left, Right, I had a good job and I Left, Right ...," on that October day we filed silently between house and cars with suitcases, lanterns, jugs of detergent, milk, bleach, and a lone can of maple syrup.

Our first afternoon there, we sat on the porch steps, and looked across the grey lake to the Franklins', a house long-abandoned and most probably haunted. After a brief caucus, we decided that after all these years of wondering, it was time to finally explore it. We piled into the boat. As my cousin Paul rowed towards the house across the lake, we girls sang. *Just you wait, 'Enry 'Iggins, Just you wait, You'll be sorry but your tears'll be too late* – shouting out the sorry, investing it with as much Cockney malice as our skinny throats could summon.

But our song faded as the boat neared shore. We scrambled up the barren rock, climbed soggy, leaf-covered steps, and pushed open the unlocked door to the Franklins' house. Splinters of fading light slanting through gaps in the walls illuminated a couch with a broken leg, spewing out mildewed stuffing. A brown, straight-backed chair had fallen on its side. An empty, greasy, blackened pan sat atop a cold wood stove. Next to it, the delicate carcass of a mouse was still clamped in its trap.

Walking cautiously through the dank room, I kicked something and looked down. A soggy game board lay littered with animal droppings, and strewn about the floor, in garish oranges and blues and greens, were the shriveled remains of popped balloons and faded Monopoly money.

Children had lived here.

Silently, we left. We girls tried singing on the boat ride back. *You'll be broke and I'll have money. Will I help you? Don't be funny.* Our song sounded like a whimper.

I was only eight and remember little of that time – just that first and last trip to a house that would never be lived in again; the sound of our parents listening to the radio; we kids playing desultory games of Sorry; the two families' dogs writhing in the damp autumn leaves.

Our house was cold and after a couple of days of awaiting the apocalypse, we decamped and went back to town.

"We probably just told you that we were taking a fun school vacation," my mother says when I ask her how she explained these events to us.

"And why were you advised to leave the city?" I press her. "Why would the Russians have bombed Montreal?"

"I don't know why he told us to leave. Maybe he thought there'd be rioting or pillaging." She pauses. "Now that I think about it, our going to the Laurentians made no sense. If anything was going to be bombed, it would have been the NORAD radar towers in Morin Heights, right near St. Adolphe."

"But you didn't realize that then?"

My mother looks perplexed. "I guess not. I don't know if we were panicked or just incredibly passive back then. It simply didn't occur to us to ask those kinds of questions."

But my parents, many parents of the 1950s and '60s, were acutely afraid and thus deeply angry in the face of such madness. This was not what so many of them had risked and lost their young lives for in World War II. Some of them managed their anxiety and rage at how their lives had shrunk so soon after blossoming, with Valium and Librium, what the Rolling Stones would later call "Mother's Little Helper." Some doubled down on their denial. They pursued stability and wealth and, when their children revolted, dismissed or, in severe cases, disowned them. And some, like my parents, looked for the other closeted malcontents who shared their restlessness.

For a few years, Jack Kennedy served as the vessel for their vague ambitions. For them and so many of their generation, JFK's inaugural address was more than lofty rhetoric. Since August 6, 1945, they'd known that, "The world is very different now. For man holds in his mortal hands the power to abolish all forms of human poverty and all forms of human life." They felt that union of hope and terror every day.

But that ended on November 22, 1963. Just before school ended that day, Mrs. Bailey told us that JFK had been shot and killed.

Susan Hirschorn and I dawdled on our walk home. It was a slow, leisurely journey, past new street signs and stop signs, each block bearing its own landmarks. *(That's the poet's house, I'd recite to myself. There's where that girl Ruth with the mustache lives. On this street used to live the man that disappeared – killed or a runaway, nobody knows.)* As we walked, we discussed what would happen next.

"Do you think the Russians will take over?" I asked Susan. As third graders born and raised in Montreal, though our airwaves were dominated by American culture and politics, we knew nothing about American laws of succession.

"They might," Susan answered. "Or they might not. I mean if they tried, the US might drop the bomb on them."

"Americans would never *start* a war," I protested.

"Wouldn't they?" she answered archly. With her brassy voice and already budding breasts, she struck me as very mature. "They're very bossy."

I'd seen televised Russians at their May Day parades. With

their jowly faces, in their square suits, they looked grumpy and mean. But they seemed too glum to terrorize anyone. In fact, they looked not so different from John Diefenbaker, until recently Canada's own petulant Prime Minister. (And his successor, Lester Pearson – well, he seemed friendly, but was named Lester and therefore couldn't be taken seriously.) Besides, it was the Americans who had dropped the two atom bombs, right?

When I got home I found my mother in the basement, crying and painting. The canvas showed faces streaked and blistered in strokes and pools of brown and beige, faces ravaged and weeping like hers. I'd never seen her use such dismal colors, or apply the brush with such sweeping violence.

We spent lots of time in the basement for the next few days, as that's where our brand new television was installed, its bulbous glass eye gazing out from the knotty pine paneling of the wall. We were there, planted on the scratchy blue couch, when Lee Harvey Oswald was escorted through the basement of the Dallas City Jail, obscured by a gauntlet of police and reporters in suits and trench coats carrying wired microphones attached to portable reel-to-reel tape recorders hanging from their shoulders. We were probably still digesting the bagels and scrambled eggs we usually had for Sunday brunch when we saw the back of a man in a hat lunge into the frame, then heard the pop of Jack Ruby's gun. Two men grabbed him and wrestled him to the ground.

"There seems to be a scuffle of some sort," an unseen broadcaster said. Then we heard cries of "He's been shot! Oswald's been shot!" Bodies crowded around something or someone, the viewers' line of sight obscured by jostling men. The correspondents gathered around Pierre, a man with a French accent who witnessed a flash coming from the gun of a man in a black hat and a brown coat. Bob Huffaker, a flustered KRLD reporter, breathlessly announced the arrival of an ambulance, the sight of the victim looking "ashen and unconscious." The video suddenly shifted to the exterior of the jail, an announcer said we'd be going "back to Harry Reasoner in New York," but we didn't. Instead, paralyzed and mesmerized, we gazed at big cars pulling out of the garage and speeding down a Dallas street.

At least that's what I imagine now, as I watch remastered footage of the event on YouTube. In one video, Oswald's right arm hangs off the stretcher and trails along the basement floor before he is hurriedly lifted into the ambulance. Bob Huffaker (who, with no earpiece to provide a guiding voice, persists in referring to the victim as "Lee Harold Oswald") struggles to be centered in the camera's frame, but police and other reporters walk to and fro in front of him as he interviews a Dallas police officer. Hands grab the jackets of those blocking the camera and yank the offending men out of the way.

"Does he look like he's dying?" Huffaker asks the officer.

A long pause. "I wouldn't want to say."

The blocked visuals, the wrong names, the dead air – it all looks so amateurish, nothing like the aerial view of O.J. Simpson's white van from the CNN helicopter in the blue sky. But on November 24th, the botched production values give events an immediacy that's re-evoked even now, over 50 years later. Millions of North Americans were sharing in the same televised experience.

It was a murder.

On November 29, 1963, after a fevered bidding contest, *Life* magazine published 30 black-and-white frames from the 26.6 second, color, eight-millimeter movie that Dallas resident Abraham Zapruder took of the presidential procession. It would become the most studied film in history. Over time, its 486 frames have been reproduced as 35 millimeter slides and as black and white photos. They've been color corrected, slowed down, and sped up. Missing frames have been identified and 16-millimeter copies of the film have been made. The Zapruder film has gotten almost six million views on YouTube, alongside the dozens of other videos showing other assassination-related footage (including one claiming to document Texas governor John Connally pulling a gun out of his jacket pocket at Love Field in preparation for shooting the President a little later on their sunny drive through Dallas).

Some conspiracy theorists denounce the Zapruder film as a fraud, buttressing their case by citing photographic consultants who point to gaps, unnatural jerkiness, and other anomalies in the film.

And today that's what we notice – the production values of the lives (and deaths) streaming to us in real time. Visual information no longer floats down to us under a brightly colored parachute; it's not snagged from mid-air by skilled and ingenious experts. It inundates us. It washes into our consciousness like a seaweed-clogged tide. Slow motion, instant replay, high definition – whether we're watching a running back dive into the end zone or a jet fly into a skyscraper, we're tempted to feel that by manipulating the image, we can understand the reality.

But back then, when Howie and I had gone looking for footprints in the newly poured concrete, events suddenly made it clear that there were big, invasive mysteries beyond our brand new sidewalks.

Who or what could be so powerful as to make our parents weep?

Children playing detective is a timeless activity, but the clues they find and the narratives they construct from them are historically specific. As kids, my parents had pretended to be rum runners and cops, Eskimos and Arctic explorers. They'd played store, enacting the most mundane transactions that signified rescue for their immigrant parents.

But my generation looked for hints to how the world worked

in the unmediated impact of real-time events. We began to recognize that adults weren't always in control, at least not the ones we knew. Old women were sent out to work by their disdainful children. Mothers and fathers got divorced. Presidents could be killed. Prisoners could be killed, even when surrounded by police.

The blocks we patrolled were like postage stamps, colorful and square-edged, rich with detail magnified by our imaginations. But beyond their borders lay train tracks and wilderness, quicksand that would swallow both the robber and Timmy if either entered it alone. There were large forces at work, glacially cold and transformative, that not even our parents understood.

Bird Skull with [ ]

by Nick Lantz

There is a hole. [	] is there, a holiness
around it, [	] holes in the medieval
mosaic [	] has been prized
by a crusader's [	] The silence left
by the birds [	] king's robe
of purple [	] feathered light
filling the abandoned [	] river.
The amphora [	] amphorafull
of museum air [	] lungs taking
in [	] atoms
of oxygen [	] patrons
took [	] studying a broken frieze
but failed to [	] passed
back into [	] The past, a kind of hole

we're always [   ] we are the hole

the past shovels [   ] into. Oh but we

are bottomless, [   ] unspooling out of us

like bright scarves. [   ] magician

turns the empty [   ] this way and that

to convince us of its [   ] *Hold on,*

we say, as a pair [   ] appear

from [   ] *Hold on, show us again.*

Waking Up

by Richard Garcia

A prose poem woke up in an alley. He was lying on the pavement among trash bins, empty bottles, cigarette butts and the smell of urine. He raised his head and noticed the rear exits to buildings. He hadn't wanted to wake up as a prose poem. He coulda been a story. Maybe just a very short story, but at least something in which something happens. He coulda been a fight or a murder or a dying child, a beautiful woman who has forgotten her name, or a soldier coming back from the war. Something. He coulda been a book of related stories in which an unnamed character, one who played no actual part in the stories, would make an appearance in each story. Perhaps he would be the unnamed character sitting, unnoticed by anyone in the story, on a park bench. Or he would deliver the mail. Or you would see him glance from the window of a departing bus. The prose poem got on his feet and dusted off his pants and the front of his shirt. He needed a shave and his teeth felt scuzzy. He knew the rear doors to the buildings were not real doors. No one would be coming to the alley. No one would pick up the garbage. It was not a real alley, but maybe it was a story — the story of his blankety-blank-blank life. Nothing would happen. He wouldn't be doing whatever he would be doing if he were a story instead of a prose poem. Damn.

The Masturbators

by J. Arthur Scott

*H*enry and his friends liked to play football when it was warm enough and dry enough outside at recess. Both sides had a dozen players at least, and routes crisscrossed the field like word match answers on Henry's homework. Their games required either total improvisation or endless huddles.

One day, Henry's friend Bryce got down on a knee in the dirt and told everybody to gather around him for one of those huddles. Henry wedged in with the rest of his team as Bryce dug something out of the pocket of his sweatshirt. Henry craned his neck over the boy in front of him and caught a mouthful of the boy's curly hair. From his spot at the center of the circle, Bryce unfolded a sheet of paper. Henry couldn't make out the creased image. He got up on tiptoes as the first giggles broke out below. Just then, the curly-haired boy ducked under Henry's arm, and sunlight caught the paper in Bryce's hands.

Henry recognized long blonde hair and the white borders of computer paper, but the rest of the image confused him. She was buck-naked. That much he could tell. And her boobs were showing.

Bryce clapped his hands closed again and the entire group collapsed in a fit of laughter. Henry didn't join in. He stood thunderstruck as bodies rolled around his legs. His teammates laughed with hands on their bellies and forearms draped across their faces, but Henry was busy trying to remember the details of the picture. The woman had been leaning back against a chair or something, and her skin looked orange. He couldn't recall much more.

"How'd you guys like the play?" Bryce asked. He stood up and the others followed his lead.

"What was that?" Henry asked.

"A naked lady. Duh!"

"But how'd you get it?"

"Found it on the computer. It's Jenny McCarthy."

Nobody said anything for a moment.

"You could get in trouble," Henry said. It just came out.

"You could get in trouble," Bryce sang, imitating him. The group broke into peals of laughter again. "What are you, a masturbator?"

Henry didn't say anything.

"You know what a masturbator is, don't you?" Bryce said. He made a gesture in the air with his thumb meeting his fingers in a loose circle.

Henry didn't know what Bryce was talking about, but he said, "Of course." Then, quickly, "Show us the picture again."

Bryce folded the page into quarters and shoved it into his pocket as the boys in the huddle watched. "That's all you're gonna get," he said. "Mrs. Green is coming, so act normal."

Everybody turned to look for Mrs. Green, who was walking around the school on recess duty. As they drifted back toward the kids with the football, somebody asked, "Remember when she got hit in the head by that soccer ball and spazzed out?" Some of the boys laughed.

"Dad said that was a seizure," Henry said, but nobody heard him.

Bryce played quarterback again and called anyone who didn't catch a pass a masturbator. Their team lost to some boys from the other fifth grade class. Afterward, Bryce said he would have shown them the picture again if they had won. Henry and Bryce had been friends since kindergarten when they had played on the tire swing together until the older kids spun them so hard they would zig sideways and fall on their face as soon as they got off. Lately, Bryce had started acting like one of the older kids, especially when they were around others, and Henry didn't know why.

At the end of the day, Bryce approached Henry as he was putting books in his backpack. "Here. You can hold on to it for now." Bryce pulled the folded picture from his pocket and dropped it into Henry's open bag.

"Bryce," Henry said. "I don't want it."

The two boys stood alone at the back of the classroom next to Henry's desk as their teacher, Mr. Willis, ushered students out the door. Mr. Willis turned and said, "You two coming?"

"Yes, Mr. Willis," Bryce said in the voice he used for teachers and parents. As they walked out of the room, Henry zipped up his backpack until the zipper bit into a fold in the canvas and got stuck. He couldn't fix the snag and walk at the same time, so he held the opening closed and shielded it from Mr. Willis as they passed him. Henry wanted to hit Bryce. Once out of earshot, Bryce turned to him and said, "Come on, Hank. Don't be a baby. Mom's been looking through my stuff."

Henry didn't want the picture. He didn't know what to do with it and was worried he'd get caught with it. He would have kept saying so, but as they reached the parking lot, Bryce was preoccupied with looking for his mother's minivan. Henry wondered if Bryce would call him a masturbator again if he tried to give the picture back.

A moment later Bryce's mother pulled into the parking lot. "See ya, Hank," Bryce said as he backpedaled away from Henry. "Mom says you and Justin can come over on Saturday if you want."

Henry fixed his backpack as he waited for his brother Lee, who took longer collecting his things at the end of the day than Henry did. Henry's first thought seeing Lee come out of the building was that Lee was lucky not to have to worry about the picture. Blooming guilt made Henry's voice sound funny when he greeted Lee, and he wondered if his brother was looking at him strangely. Henry fixated on the picture as they walked, even as Lee described how somebody brought a cat skeleton to class and how a new girl had told him that she had never seen Power Rangers before. "Can you believe it?" Lee asked, and Henry said that he couldn't. Henry imagined the square of paper shuffling down through the things in his backpack. He hoped it made it all the way to the bottom, like when he sank to the mesh floor of the McDonald's ball pit as other kids jostled above him.

He thought about how he would hide the picture when he got home. He would either stash it in a pile of *Sports Illustrated for Kids* issues in his closet, or he would put it under his mattress. It would have been the kind of thing to hide under a loose floorboard—like in the movies—but his house was too new for loose floorboards and his bedroom was carpeted. Lee would sometimes sneak into Henry's room to cut photos of his favorite athletes from the magazines for collages he made on construction paper with glue sticks. So Henry first thought to hide the picture under his mattress. But he didn't know when his father would be coming for his sheets. When his mother was still alive, Henry had helped her with the laundry on Saturdays, but his father didn't stick to a schedule. There were just some days when he would overturn the house in a frenzy of chores. If Lee found the picture he might tell on Henry, but there was a chance he wouldn't if Henry let him look at it. Henry didn't even want to think of his father finding it.

Once they arrived home, Henry had to wait for Lee to use the bathroom before he could run to his closet to hide the picture. He risked a quick look and this time was able to process its details. JM—as Henry code-named her in his mind—had large, round breasts with nipples that were much wider than Henry's own, or even his father's. She wore fancy black socks that came up to the middle of her thighs, and there was a strip of hair between her legs that was much darker than the hair tumbling down her shoulders. Henry felt a dizziness he had never felt before. He couldn't tell what color her eyes were, but he felt his own drawn to them. She wasn't smiling; not really. She was between faces. Like someone had told her to smile and she had only made it halfway there before the person took the photo. Henry wondered whether the cushions beneath her were stiff like the pillows in the guest bedroom. Maybe she was uncomfortable.

Henry remembered Lee and hurried to hide the picture. He pulled an issue of *Sports Illustrated for Kids* from his stack, but the cover had Michael Jordan on it. He reached for a different one: Ken Griffey, Jr. Baseball didn't interest Lee. Henry found two pages without photos, and then realized the other sides of the pages couldn't have photographs either. He didn't have time to find four in a row without photos, so he settled on three toward the back and shoved the paper into the spine of the magazine. He steadied the top of the stack with his palm and slid the issue back into place toward the middle just as Lee banged out of the bathroom.

Later that night, Henry brought the family dictionary into the guest room while his father was watching TV and Lee was drying dishes. Henry tried to look up "masturbator" but couldn't figure out the spelling and had to search down through the M's. He found "masturbate" and read its definition: "to stimulate one's genitals with one's hand for sexual pleasure." Henry didn't know what "stimulate" meant but had heard grown-ups use it. He didn't know "genitals" either, and he thought of gizzard and gonad, other words adults used. He kept reading the line over. His anticipation would build until he reached the phrase "sexual pleasure." It felt wrong to read those words; worse yet to dwell on them. He returned the dictionary to its place in the den and repeated the definition under his breath until he could recite it like the naughty sounding commandments from Sunday school.

Henry spent the rest of the week sneaking moments with JM every chance he got. The folds of the paper began to swing freely like hinges and wore lines across the image. Luckily they didn't ruin any of the good parts. Henry would look at JM's breasts and privates and struggle to take in both at once. His vision would double if he stared for too long, and he would have to shake his head and blink. Then he would hear a noise and it was back to page forty-one for JM and back to the stack for Ken Griffey, Jr.

It got so that Henry couldn't resist running to the closet the minute he was alone. When he went to sleep he stashed the picture and a penlight between his sheets and would awaken the next morning still clutching the paper under his pillow with the penlight at his feet or on the floor. He would smooth JM out and kiss each of her breasts before hiding her again. Kissing her sent soda bubbles crawling up his bones.

That Saturday, when Henry rode his bicycle to Bryce's house, JM rode in his pocket. Bryce's dad was waxing his Chevy Silverado in the driveway. He did that every weekend, or at least every weekend Henry was there. Henry said hello and Bryce's dad waved but didn't look up from the cloudy film on the truck as Henry went inside through the garage.

Justin was already there. He lived closer to Bryce than Henry did, and Henry felt a pang of jealousy seeing them together. They were playing loud music that sounded like lumberjack saws bending back and forth, and Bryce and Justin were taking turns jumping off the couch and rolling across the floor.

"Hey guys," Henry shouted.

"Hey," Justin said.

Bryce was too busy jumping around to respond. A decorative plate fell off a shelf onto the carpet without breaking.

"We're head-banging," Justin said.

"What's this song?" Henry asked.

"What?"

"Nothing."

Justin nudged Bryce. "Can we try a chat room now?"

Bryce nodded and turned to Henry. "Did you bring my picture?"

"Yeah," Henry said. He pulled out JM and handed her to Bryce.

"Aw man, look how messed up it is. What have you been doing with it?"

Henry stared at JM in Bryce's hands and didn't like how Bryce held her. "Nothing," he said.

"Yeah right," Bryce said. "Hank and Jenny sittin' in a tree, H-U-M-P-I-N-G." Bryce made the masturbator gesture with his hand again and laughed. "Come on. Let's go see if any girls will cyber."

Henry followed Bryce and Justin back to Bryce's computer room. Bryce's mother must have been running errands. Bryce's family was repainting the room, so all of the furniture other than the desk and chair had been removed and a sheet of plastic covered most of the carpet. Bryce sat at the desk and Henry and Justin leaned over his shoulders.

"Last night Justin and I cybered with two high school girls from Texas," Bryce said. Henry felt the pang again—he hadn't known they were hanging out the night before. "We told them we were exchange students from Australia and they totally bought it. Right, Justin?"

"Fuckin' A," Justin said. He had started saying that, but Henry didn't know what the "A" meant.

"Think any of them will cyber with us today?" Henry asked.

Bryce didn't answer, because Justin had started saying the word "Barbie" in an Australian accent. They both started saying it and laughing, but Henry didn't know why. He thought about Barbie dolls and wondered what they had to do with Australia.

As the three of them listened to the computer dialing up, Bryce asked, "What should our name be?"

Justin suggested "The Hockey Guys."

"That's stupid," Bryce said.

Nobody said anything for a moment, so Henry said, "The Masturbators."

Justin laughed, but Bryce said, "What are you talking about? You don't even know what a masturbator is."

"Do too," Henry said.

"Then what is it?" Bryce asked. He swiveled his chair around to face Henry. Justin leaned back against the desk and looked around the room without meeting Henry's eyes.

"It's when you stimulate one's genitals."

Bryce blew air through his lips and laughed with a huff. "You're such a moron. That's not what masturbating is."

"Is too. It's in the dictionary."

Bryce said, "No it's not. Masturbating is when you pull on your wiener. My babysitter told me, and he's in high school so he would know. He says that middle school is full of masturbators."

"That doesn't even make sense," Henry said. "Pulling on your wiener hurts."

"See," Bryce shouted, "you have been masturbating!" Bryce slapped Justin on the shoulder. "And duh, Hank. Of course it hurts. That's why it's a bad thing." Justin laughed with Bryce, but Henry thought he was faking it. Henry wished Justin would say something to change the subject, but he just said, "Fuckin' A."

"Then why are there so many middle schoolers pulling their wieners?" Henry asked.

"How should I know?" Bryce asked. He suddenly sounded bored and turned back to the computer. "Such a masturbator," he muttered. "We're going to be called "Justin Jagr," and we're going to tell girls that we're Jaromir Jagr's brother."

"They're never going to believe that," Henry said. "And why are we using Justin's name?"

"I don't mind," Justin said.

"Because it's more believable if you use a real name, and because he's not being a masturbator." Bryce said. He started typing "ASL?" in messages to usernames that sounded like girls. Henry knew that ASL meant "age, sex, location."

As they waited for a response, the door to the garage opened in the kitchen, and Bryce's dad shouted across the house for Bryce to turn down the music. They heard him open the refrigerator. Glass tinkled. Probably a Miller High Life. He always drank High Lifes when he worked on his truck. "And you better not be on the internet. You hear me? I'm waiting for a call about my shift."

Bryce disconnected and turned off the monitor. "We're not," he shouted. He grinned at Justin and Henry as he left the room to turn down the stereo. Henry and Justin could hear Bryce's father say, "Bullshit, you're not. If your mother catches you again, she'll be up my ass, so knock it off." There was a pause as Bryce said something that Henry and Justin couldn't hear.

"I don't care," Bryce's father said. "Go outside and stay out of trouble or you're not getting new goalie pads. End of story."

The music cut out, and they could hear Bryce protesting, which embarrassed Henry as he and Justin stared at their reflections in the computer monitor.

"Enough," Bryce's father said. Then the door thumped closed.

Henry and Justin walked out into the hallway to find Bryce as Bryce's father cracked the door open again and called out, "Did your mother say when she'd be home?"

"No," Bryce said.

"Come get me if work calls."

Justin had to leave to watch his sister's soccer game. After he left, Henry paced around the living room. Bryce lay back across an ottoman with his head hanging upside down. His face slowly darkened. He didn't say anything. Henry grew antsy and went to the kitchen.

"Can I have a Dew?" he called out, but Bryce didn't answer.

When Henry walked back into the living room, Bryce was sitting right side up again. "You know what we should do?" Bryce asked.

"What?"

"We should burn the picture so Mom doesn't find it."

Henry felt all the bubbles in his body boil at once and considered stealing JM from Bryce. But the relief of no longer having to hide her and the excitement of starting a fire slowly replaced his anger.

"How'll we do it?" Henry asked.

"Mom and Dad have matches in the medicine cabinet," Bryce said. He left the living room as Henry sat down on the couch. A clock on the wall ticked loudly behind him, and he could hear a radio playing oldies in the garage.

Bryce came back and waved Henry up. They snuck out the back door of the kitchen and walked across a patio to a grill under a tree along the rear wall of the house. The grill's cover lay in a heap to one side. Bryce handed Henry the picture and matches and ran around the house to check on his father. Henry felt better without Justin around. He liked how Bryce spoke to him directly when they were alone. He liked how Bryce laughed at his jokes.

When Bryce returned, he lifted up the lid of the grill and took the picture from Henry. Bryce unfolded it and set it down on the metal rack, where it lay open and creased at its folds. Henry clasped his hands together, nudged Bryce with his elbow until Bryce copied him, and said, "We come here today to say goodbye to this naked lady named Jenny McCarthy."

Bryce started snickering, and Henry went on, "We're all going to miss looking at her, and her big ole jugs." Bryce cracked up. "Except for Mr. Willis, who's probably never even seen a naked lady before."

"What a lame-o," Bryce said, and Henry felt a rush of confidence.

"Is there anything you'd like to say, Bryce?" Henry asked.

"Yes," Bryce said, joining in the game and quickly bringing himself near to tears. "I-I-I," he stuttered. "I would just like to say, 'Goodbye, my darling! And goodbye to your big bazongas!'" Henry fell down laughing, and Bryce hollered, "Your big bazooka bazongas!"

Henry picked some clover blossoms from the grass and stood up and laid one on each of JM's breasts. Bryce pulled out a match and started flicking it on the box. He tried twice before the head flew off. "Damnit," he said, and he threw the spoiled match into a metal pail near the grill. "You try." Bryce handed the matchbox to Henry.

Henry had never held a match before. He held the stick between his thumb and index finger like Bryce had done and scraped the match head against the red sandpaper stuff on the box. The match flared in a plume. He stared at it as it welled up and then settled into a small nub of flame.

"Nice one," Bryce said. "Quick, before it goes out."

Henry imitated his father lighting newspaper scraps for campfires. He held the flame under the edge of the picture until it caught. He kept holding on until its heat bit into the meat of his fingers. Then he dropped the match and shook his hand in the air.

The boys stood shoulder-to-shoulder watching the picture burn. The fire ate the paper in a steady orange wave that curled JM's body into a black crescent as it disappeared. The clover blossoms blackened and fell to the bottom of the grill without fully burning, but the picture was reduced to charred flakes. Bryce lifted the rack with one hand and picked up the larger pieces. Then Henry helped him close the grill and they carried what was left of the picture to the back of the yard to scatter under a row of evergreen hedges. They each took turns consoling the other with pats on the back as the other wailed and grieved.

On Tuesday night the following week, Henry and Lee arrived home from school to find their father pulling a pizza out of the oven. He was still wearing a tie and loafers, so the boys knew he would be leaving soon, probably for a work dinner. He paused to hug them and gave Lee a peck on the top of his head. Then he ushered them to stools at the kitchen island and transferred the pizza to a cutting board on the counter in front of them. He cut the pizza with a big butcher knife, because he hated cleaning the wheeled cutter. He spun around to head upstairs and said over his shoulder, "Hank, grab the parmesan cheese from the fridge and a juice box for you and your brother." He was up the stairs now and called out, "Lee, you better use a napkin."

Lee had a slice and a half and then wandered off to the dining room to resume a battle of Ninja Turtles and G.I. Joes. Henry had three slices and was biting into a fourth when his father came back.

He had removed his tie and put something in his hair. He smelled like aftershave. Henry watched him pick up keys and his wallet from the corner of the counter.

"Your cousin Corey should be here in a minute. You're in charge of watching Lee until he gets here, Hank. No video games tonight. Uh uh, no interrupting. You played enough last night. And no friends over. You can be outside until it starts to get dark and then I want you both inside and your homework done before bed. Nine-thirty. Nine for Lee. No staying up with Corey to watch movies again. I don't want to hear about any more nightmares."

Henry's father gathered up his stuff from the counter as he spoke and walked to the front door. "Come give me a hug. Then I gotta go."

Henry hugged him and heard Lee shout, "Bye, Dad." Then his father walked out to the Buick at the curb and drove off. Henry could hear Lee making shooting noises and then karate noises and then more shooting noises. The G.I. Joes seemed to have the upper hand.

Corey arrived as Henry was throwing a football to himself in the front yard. Corey was an eighth grader and rode a mountain bike, not a BMX like Henry and his friends did. Corey leaned the bike against a tree and said, "How's it going, Hank?"

"Pretty good."

"Your dad still here?"

"No, he had to leave. Lee's inside."

Corey put his hands out for a pass and Henry threw him the ball.

"Nice spiral," Corey said. "Try throwing it lower, like a laser beam." Corey tossed Henry the ball, and Henry wound up for a harder throw. He lost control, and it bounced off the ground at Corey's feet. "Good power. Coach says the trick is keeping your aim on hard throws."

They threw the ball back and forth for a while, but Henry never made it fly like a laser beam. He wanted to ask his cousin if he knew about masturbating. Corey was old enough to know about that stuff and wouldn't tell on Henry. But a sense of shame tightened around Henry's stomach every time he started to ask and the question stuck on his lips.

"Alright," Corey said, "I need to check on Lee and call Jessica. He flipped the ball back to Henry underhanded and walked toward the house.

Henry hurried to catch up. "Who's Jessica?"

"My new girlfriend," Corey said. "Jessica Price. She's on the volleyball team. She's had a crush on me since like sixth grade camp."

"Have you kissed her?" Henry asked.

"Of course."

Corey reached the front door and Henry blurted out, "What does masturbator mean?"

Corey took his hand off the screen door and snorted. "Where'd you hear that?"

"Bryce Grant told us about it at school. He says it means pulling on your wiener, but the dictionary says it means when you stimulate one's genitals."

"That's, well, that's both kind of right," Corey said. "But it's pronounced 'genitals.'" He emphasized the soft G.

"Oh," Henry said. "Have you and Jessica Price masturbated?"

Corey started laughing, but not unkindly. "You don't masturbate with someone else. Besides, girls don't masturbate." He paused and Henry turned back and forth in place, eyeing his shoes as they pivoted in the grass. "Don't let Bryce mess with you. He probably doesn't know anything about it."

Henry felt embarrassed about mispronouncing "genitals" and just as confused about masturbating as before. But Corey punched him lightly on the arm as he went inside. Henry was glad he had asked.

Corey stood at the kitchen counter most of the night on the phone with Jessica Price, twisting the telephone cord until it coiled up to his elbow.

Henry and Lee watched "Home Improvement" while Corey was on the phone. Then they all watched a Discovery Channel special on cheetahs. Later, Henry helped Corey put Lee to bed.

When they were back downstairs, Corey switched to "Nick at Night" and they watched "The Munsters" for a while. During a commercial break, Corey said to Henry, "If Bryce teases you about sex words, just ask him if he knows what '69' means."

"What do you mean?"

"Like when you 69 with a girl. No way Bryce knows about that."

"What's 69?"

"Look," Corey said, grabbing a *TV Guide* and a pen from the coffee table. "69'ing is when a boy and a girl are like this." He drew the number 69 on the back cover of the *TV Guide*. Then he ran his pen around the 6 again from bottom to top. "See, this is the head and this is the rest of the body." Then he ran his pen around the 9 again from top to bottom. "And this is the other person's body. Get it?"

Henry didn't get it.

"Then, ya know, they do it, and that's 69'ing."

Henry stared at the number on the magazine and tried to figure out what Corey meant. Corey reached for the *TV Guide* and ripped off the part of the cover that he had used for the drawing. Then, seeing that the pen had imprinted the number on the next few pages as well, he tore off more corners until he couldn't make out the number anymore.

"By the way, don't tell anybody about me and Jessica," Corey said as he turned to face the television again. "She has to dump Lunchbox before we're official."

"Who's Lunchbox?" Henry asked.

"I mean it, Hank."

The next weekend Bryce and Justin came over to Henry's house to play roller hockey in the street. Later, after dinner, they started talking about a sleepover, the way they always would when it got late and nobody wanted to go home. Sleepovers meant games of kick the can and ghost in the graveyard. They meant hall hockey tournaments with four players, even if Henry had to play with Lee on his team. They meant staying up late and trying to prank the person who fell asleep first.

Henry's father thought it over and finally agreed when Henry started to beg. They followed the usual procedure: Bryce and Justin took turns calling home and asking, mentioning that the other was staying too, saying that they would behave and that Mr. Harver had enough sleeping bags and that Henry had extra pajamas they could borrow and that they could brush their teeth with their finger just this once.

Around ten o'clock Henry's father went upstairs and told them to behave themselves because he didn't want to have to come back down. They all said goodnight and then went back to paging through Henry's fourth grade yearbook picking out the prettiest girls. Justin went upstairs to the kitchen on a mission for Oreos. He was gone a long time, and Bryce and Henry looked up expectantly from the yearbook when he started back down the stairs to the living room.

Justin had his hands behind his back, and when he pulled them out, he didn't have cookies but rather a plastic videocassette case from the rental store. It was a double case, the kind for really long movies. Justin held it up to Henry and Bryce's puzzled expressions.

"What's that?" Bryce asked.

"Guess," Justin said.

"*Dances with Wolves*?" Henry asked. Henry's father would sometimes rent that movie, or *Braveheart*, and they both came with two tapes like that. Henry wished he had said *Braveheart* instead.

Bryce started laughing. "That movie sounds stupid."

"It's not that," Justin said. He slid down next to them and showed them the case. "It's *Titanic*," he whispered.

Bryce and Henry exchanged looks and Bryce rolled over, stifling a whoop. Even Henry knew about *Titanic*. He had heard that a lady got naked in it. His father must have rented it and left it on the counter next to his wallet and keys so that he would remember to return it.

"You shouldn't have took that," Henry whispered to Justin. "What if my dad catches us?"

"But he's sleeping," Justin whispered.

"Yeah, he's sleeping, Hank," Bryce said.

Henry knew his father wasn't sleeping, but he also knew that he wouldn't come downstairs unless the boys were making noise. "Ok," Henry said at last. "We can watch, but we need to stay real quiet."

Henry turned out the overhead light. Justin opened the case as Bryce did a couple silent somersaults, stood up dizzy, and crashed into the couch. Henry shushed Bryce. He grabbed the remote control for the television and hit the power button and the down volume button in quick succession. Then he turned to channel three, fed the tape into the VCR, and hit fast forward.

What seemed like an eternity later, Henry pressed play amid stifled commotion from Bryce and Justin alerting him that they had reached the scene. The two of them were lying on their stomachs in sleeping bags facing the television with their chins stilted on top their palms. "Shh," Henry said over his shoulder. He knelt next to the VCR and paused the tape to look up at the screen.

"Fuckin' A," Justin whispered.

"They're okay," Bryce said. He rolled over to look at them upside down.

"They're better than okay," Justin said in protest.

"Jenny McCarthy's were bigger."

"So what?" Justin said, a little too loudly.

"Quiet, guys," Henry said. "My dad will hear."

Justin said, "You're just jealous because I had the idea and you didn't."

"Nuh-uh," Bryce said. "I don't even care about that. I just like Jenny McCarthy's boobs better."

Henry shushed them again, but Justin and Bryce paid no attention.

"What makes you the expert?" Justin asked.

"Because I've cybered, like, a million more girls than you," Bryce shouted.

Henry exploded in a hiss. "Shut up, both of you. You're going to get us in trouble when Dad wakes up." Bryce and Justin turned to look at Henry as he kept talking. "You didn't even have JM as long as I did, Bryce. You think you're so cool because you know what masturbating is and you cyber and stuff. But I bet you don't know what 69 means."

Bryce said, "That's not even a thing. And what's JM?"

"Is too a thing! Corey told me all about it. And you don't know."

"So what. 69 is probably for losers. Doesn't your cousin have anything better to do than talk to you about stupid numbers?" Bryce turned over in his sleeping bag. "This movie is boring. I'm going to sleep."

"You wouldn't say that if you were the one who knew about 69," Henry said. "You would think it was cool."

"Yeah," Justin said. "Hank's right. You're always…"

The floor creaked loudly above their heads, followed by heavy footsteps.

"Shh," Henry said. He spun back toward the television, but his momentum carried his face up against the glass, shocking his nose with static. He pulled his head back and realized he was staring at breasts. His eyes went unfocused at the nearness of the image, and he sat there dazed for a moment before trying to jab the power button on the television. His finger mashed the volume button instead, and the pop and fizzle of the paused video rose from the speakers as Henry's father came down the stairs and Henry turned to face him. He was vaguely aware of Bryce pretending to be asleep in his sleeping bag and Justin looking back and forth from Henry to his father. Henry's father scanned the darkened room by the glow of the television and turned to Henry. "What's going on down here? You know you're not allowed to watch this, Henry."

"We were just…" Henry said.

"I told the three of you to behave and be quiet, and I meant it. Now turn that off and go to sleep, and we'll talk about this in the morning."

"It's my fault, Mr. Harver," Justin said.

Henry's father looked at Justin, then at Henry, and then at Bryce lying in his sleeping bag. He turned around and started climbing the stairs. "Go to bed, boys."

Henry awoke to a noise in the night and looked around in confusion. After his father left, they had ejected the tape and gone to sleep without talking. It was too dark to make out more than shapes in the room. Justin was a mound of sleeping bag on the couch, but Bryce's bag was flat on the carpet. Henry could see a faint light from the kitchen upstairs and heard voices. He crawled out of his sleeping bag and crept over to the stairs.

"…bother you, Roxanne, but he says he wants to come home.

I tried to sit with him again, but it's no use."

There was a pause, and Henry thought he heard a sniffle. Then his father said, "Thanks. I'd bring him myself, but the others can't be here alone." Another pause. "Okay then. See you in a bit." Henry heard his father hang up and then say softly, "You can't keep doing this, Bryce. If you want to sleep over, you have to stay the whole night. Do you want some chocolate milk?"

Henry found his sleeping bag again as he heard the refrigerator open. He lay down and turned toward the couch. Justin was awake. His eyes caught the light from upstairs.

"What's going on?" Justin whispered. "Is Bryce going home again?"

"Yeah," Henry said.

"He's such a baby. I'm glad he's leaving."

Henry smiled and crossed his arms behind his head on the pillow.

"What does 69 mean?" Justin asked.

"I don't really know," Henry said.

"Is it a real thing?"

"Yeah. Corey said so. But I don't know what he was talking about. He just drew the number and kept pointing at it with a pen."

"Hmm."

Henry thought about it and nestled further into his sleeping bag. "I think it's when you sleep in the opposite direction of somebody in bed. Like with your feet next to their head. And that's what the numbers mean."

"The numbers?"

"The six and the nine are the people in bed because the round parts are their heads."

"Oh."

"So, like, you 69 when you do that," Henry said.

"Like with your brother when you're camping? That's not

cool."

"Yeah, I don't get it either. Maybe it's only sexy with a girl."

"Huh." Justin turned in his sleeping bag. They heard Bryce's mother pull into the driveway in her minivan and the front door of the house open and close. A minute later the kitchen light went out and they heard footsteps cross the ceiling again. After a while Justin said, "I'm sorry I got you in trouble, Hank."

Henry stared at the ceiling. He had forgotten about having to talk to his father in the morning, and shame crept back into his stomach. "It's okay," he said.

"Goodnight."

"'Night."

Sleep set in slowly, but eventually it took them both. Henry even made sure to keep his hands inside his sleeping bag in case Justin tried dipping his fingers in warm water to make him pee. Bryce had told them how to do it, and he claimed it worked every time.

Passport to Brooklyn

by Enzo Silon Surin

Have you forgotten which bus takes you
down Flatbush Avenue—ballpark where
on Saturday afternoons, a beer-bellied
mechanic rounded the bases all the way
home—your no-hitter stashed in his pocket?

Have you forgotten buying knock-offs
and bootlegged mix-tapes on Jamaica Ave,
nights spent crushing cardboard in the back-
room of Payless with the Dread—late night
dollar-cab rides—beef patty, champagne

cola on your breath—the whims and warps
of New York City potholes? The flavor
of quarter-waters staled when you tried to
unlearn the same strut that made Danielle
wanna have your baby—it kept even real

thugs at bay. You have forgotten nights,
riding shotgun in Shawn's Peugeot—
daydreams of Rose's sister—two years
younger, a poet—who at fourteen, spell-
bound you to her doorstep, long after

lights would bail. Streets of whatever city—
names you no longer recognize—no matter
what corner you're on—when you can't
seem to find a good bodega or the way back,
find the vial of scented oil in your pocket

—flicking the cap's dull black enamel—
the one Frankie gifted the year Wu Tang
Clan's Protect Ya Neck bellowed from
his headphones in the back of English—
the year before he was stabbed to death.

The Promise of Magdoos:

A Sliver of Hope in the Syrian Refugee Crisis

by Merissa Khurma

A Jordanian woman in the Northeastern city of Mafraq had been nagging her husband for weeks to take her to the Za'atari refugee camp. Her request was a simple one, *Magdoos*, baby eggplants stuffed with walnuts and sun-dried red peppers and pickled in olive oil and garlic. A prominent Syrian staple for breakfast and dinner, these mouthwatering eggplants are often prepared at home in autumn, then preserved in traditional jars and consumed all year long. The Za'atari camp was now home to the best Syrian-made *Magdoos*. Disgruntledly, the husband finally caved and the Jordanian couple started their ten-kilometer journey to the camp, in search of the Syrian specialty.

The third largest refugee camp worldwide, Za'atari is home to more than 80,000 Syrian refugees today. Divided into twelve districts with tents, one-room prefabricated housing units, football pitches, playgrounds and a bustling market street, Za'atari has morphed into an informal city. In population terms, it is Jordan's fourth largest city. "We built a camp and the Syrians built a city," is a phrase often heard amongst politicos and opinion leaders in the more developed and modernized Jordanian capital. More than seventy kilometers from Amman and thirteen kilometers from the Jordanian-Syrian border, the Za'atari camp may resemble a shantytown, but according to the world's refugee agency, UNHCR, its economy generates around 14 million dollars every month. In addition to the delectable Syrian *Magdoos*, Za'atari's market street, known as the 'Champs-Elysees,' offers a plethora of products. Some goods are produced in the camp, primarily food, beverages and traditional textiles, and others are traded with Jordanian towns near by.

While it remains surrounded by barbed wire and guarded by Jordanian security forces, "Za'atari still has a soul," reflecting the resilience of the Syrian people, says Andrew Harper, UNHCR head in Jordan. "The refugee response has worked thus far," he adds; however, five years into the Syrian conflict and the refugee crisis, Syrians "are losing hope and sense of purpose." Similarly, Jordan, the third largest host country after Lebanon and Turkey, with more than a million Syrians, is still struggling to adequately address the myriad challenges associated with the influx of refugees. It is not merely a transient refugee crisis. It is a long-term and complicated reality particularly given Jordan's already challenging political and economic conditions. Surrounded by turbulent conflict and ISIS threats, Jordan's economy is lagging behind with slow GDP growth at 2.4%, high unemployment at 13%, and a state budget deficit of 1.3 billion dollars in 2015. The closure of land-trading routes with Syria and Iraq has adversely impacted Jordan's trade, especially given that both neighboring countries have traditionally been its largest trading partners. Regional conflict and the general perception of insecurity associated with the Middle East have also affected tourism, one of Jordan's key sectors. This reality, compounded by the UNHCR statistic that it takes 17 years on average for a refugee to return to their home country, underlines the severity of Jordan's predicament.

More than a jar of Magdoos

The Jordanian husband waited impatiently in the car as his wife dashed enthusiastically into the *Magdoos* haven; a decorated prefab home attached to a UNHCR tent. A white-bearded Syrian man approached the car, accompanied by a young woman whose innocent face was covered by a *niqab*, often worn by ultra-conservative Muslim women. The two men barely exchanged pleasantries before the white bearded elder offered his young daughter. She unveiled her beautiful face to the perfect Jordanian stranger and the deal was sealed. Within moments, the teenage Syrian girl not only became a bride, but another good, sold in the thriving Za'atari market. As distasteful as it is, the likes of this child bride transaction have been on the rise alarmingly amongst the Syrian refugee population in Jordan since the beginning of the conflict in 2011. According to a UNICEF report, the percentage of registered Syrian child marriages, under the age of eighteen, increased from 12% in 2011 to more than 30% in 2014. This surge reveals that the pressures of displacement and economic hardship experienced by Syrians are driving families to marry their daughters at an early stage. In fact, various international assessments of the situation in Jordan converge around poverty and lack of unemployment amongst Syrians as a major contributing factor to the rise of child marriages. Other reasons cited by the studies include low levels of education, conservative religious or cultural views, and 'compelling circumstances' such as sexual abuse or pregnancy.

Bound Together

The Jordanian wife returned to the car with a jar of *Magdoos* and a wide smile painted across her face. She noticed the young lady settled in the back seat; her smile withered away as her husband started the engine. "We are giving her a lift to Mafraq city," he claimed. It was not until they returned to their modest abode that he introduced his Jordanian wife to his new Syrian bride. "How can we afford this?" bewailed the Jordanian wife; end of story. This story was circulated widely, particularly amongst Jordanian women of Mafraq, worried about their husbands and families amidst rising rates of Syrian child marriages. While marrying a second wife is legal and acceptable in Jordan, it is neither the norm nor is it celebrated akin to other Muslim societies in the region. Any marriage should also be officiated by a sheikh, however, according to the UNICEF report, Syrian refugees in Jordan "are reportedly accepting that this role be performed by a stranger," which in many cases increases the risk that these marriages are not conducted in "good faith."

The fate of this particular young Syrian bride is unknown. However, the stories of other young Syrian brides across Jordan illustrate a painful reality. "I got married at the age of thirteen. I never really had the chance to get to know my husband until his family wanted him to marry me," recounted Hania, a fifteen-year-old Syrian girl, according to a Save the Children report. Reem, also fifteen, said she feels "sad when I see other girls from my neighborhood going to school. Whenever I see a woman who has become a doctor or a lawyer or has finished her education, I get upset."

This captures the essence of the challenge faced by both Syrian refugees and their Jordanian hosts, not only regarding early marriage, but also the impact on the girls' future, the families and community. Particularly in Mafraq, where the Syrian refugees outnumber their Jordanian local hosts, it is a reminder that both communities' future is bound together. It is also a window into the severity of the socioeconomic situation facing both Syrians and Jordanians; a dual challenge for the Government of Jordan as the Syrian conflict enters its fifth year.

"It is essential to think about both refugees and host communities, especially the poorer communities of northern Jordan," notes Curtis Ryan, an expert on Jordanian and Middle East politics. "Any move beyond crisis, and toward longer term support and development is worth trying," he adds. The Government of Jordan is certainly moving in this direction.

At the London donor conference for the Syrian refugee crisis in January 2016, the Jordanian government issued a statement, referred to as the "Jordan Compact," outlining a creative and collaborative approach between the government and the international community to addressing the Syrian refugee challenge. The plan focuses on turning the refugee crisis into an opportunity for development. This newly recalibrated policy entails addressing the needs of local host communities and building their resilience, attracting new foreign direct investment, and preferential access to the European Union's market for Jordanian exports. More importantly, this new thinking includes creating 200,000 jobs for Syrians, according to Imad Fakhoury, Jordan's Minister of Planning and International Cooperation. However, issuing work permits for Syrians, while beneficial for both refugees and the host country, is also "politically complicated, at a time when a part of Jordanian society is hypersensitive to demographic changes and identity politics," remarks Ryan. These concerns can certainly be assuaged, though, by creating jobs for Jordanians as outlined in the Jordan Compact. Moreover, according to a report issued by the International Labor Organization (ILO), despite the increase of informal Syrian refugee economic activity in four principal governorates hosting the largest number of Syrians (Irbid, Mafraq, Zarqa and Amman), "there is little change in the total number of economically active Jordanians there." The ILO report also reveals that Syrian workers in agriculture, construction and other sectors known to be less attractive to Jordanians, have had a more negative impact on migrant workers who normally occupy these jobs.

Getting to Work

Praised by UN Resident and Humanitarian Coordinator Edward Kallon as a "bold and innovative" framework, the Jordan Compact is also questioned by opinion leaders as an overly ambitious plan especially given the country's economic and political difficult reality.

"Jordan needs to grow at approximately 8% per annum over a minimum of five years in order to gradually create the announced 200,000 thousand jobs for Syrians, without increasing the local unemployment rate," argues Omar Razzaz, who chairs the Jordan Strategy Forum, an Amman-based, economics-focused think tank. A sobering assessment in light of the 2.4% growth Jordan's economy has witnessed amidst difficult regional conditions. Razzaz adds that creating employment opportunities requires a fresh look at the Jordanian labor market context and the structure of the local economy. With an attractive promise from the EU under the Jordan Compact regarding lifting tariffs on Jordanian exports, efforts must be focused on "restructuring the economy towards exports especially outside of the Middle East region," Razzaz argues, adding emphatically that "we have no choice but to get it right."

To date, local newspapers report that Jordan has received pledges worth 1.7 billion dollars in grants to fund its new developmental approach to the Syrian refugee crisis. Some of this funding will go into the establishment of five new development zones where 50% to 70% of the jobs would be given to Syrians and the rest to Jordanians. These zones will not only take time to be up and running, they also require more than the dollars pledged in new investments to create the 200,000 jobs announced by the Government of Jordan. Secretary General of Jordan's Ministry of Planning and International Cooperation Saleh al-Kharabsheh told the

Guardian newspaper after the London conference that even if you "attract new investments of $2bn," you may be able to create "tens of thousands of jobs," but not 200,000. It is a colossal challenge.

Nevertheless, providing economic opportunities for Syrians as outlined in the Jordan Compact represents the only way forward. In addition to alleviating pressures on the Government of Jordan and addressing the deteriorating conditions of local host communities, it would also lessen the dependence on humanitarian aid, which has been dwindling in the past two years. In 2015, a mere 45% of UNHCR's financial needs were met by the international donor community, leading many displaced Syrians in the major frontline states, including Jordan, to embark on wobbly rubber boats into uncharted waters. For more than 2,000 refugees, that was their last journey.

As UNHCR's Harper noted, beyond the services provided that keep people alive, Syrians need to work, educate their children and have a "sense of purpose" for the future. UNHCR is certainly doing its part in coordination with the Government of Jordan to facilitate implementation of the Jordan Compact initiative. In April 2016, the refugee agency in Amman launched a pilot project to "help 2,000 Syrians get jobs in the export garment sector, as a partner of the 'Better Work Jordan' program," run by the ILO, according to a press statement. Additionally, UNHCR is organizing "job fairs for Syrian refugees in community centers close to the relevant industrial zones," noted the statement.

Such collaborative efforts are crucial to ensuring a successful fruition of the Government of Jordan's innovative and ambitious plan. Getting Syrians and unemployed Jordanians to work is a lengthy process that requires coordination and alignment of Jordan's economic reforms and continued support from the international community, both governmental and non-governmental entities.

Five years into this largest humanitarian and refugee crisis, UN High Commissioner for Refugees Filippo Grandi offered a sobering message to all involved: "If the world fails to work together due to short-term interests, lack of courage and knee-jerk reactions to shift the burden elsewhere, we will look back ruefully on this lost opportunity to act with solidarity and shared humanity."

The Jordan Compact is no magical formula to the Syrian crisis. But it is the last best chance to inject a sense of normalcy and raise hope for a desperate yet resilient displaced Syrian population. It is an opportunity to act with "shared humanity" and to strengthen the social fabric of Jordanian society that has been adversely affected as well. If implemented correctly, the promise is that the young Syrian bride in the *Magdoos* story would dare to imagine a bright future for herself and her children. The promise is also that the Jordanian couple whose fate changed dramatically with a jar of *Magdoos*, would also have a chance to rebuild their familial bonds and to also give their children an opportunity to realize their aspirations.

THE KING DIED AND THEN THE QUEEN DIED

by Maggie Smith

E.M. Forster's definition of plot is less about plot
than the length of narrative you drag around.
You hear it all the time: after sixty years of marriage,
one dies of something more or less tangible,
and months later, the other. When you go, I'll follow
but not too closely. They wrote *strong* on my chart
when my heart stopped keeping time, and when
for ten full minutes I couldn't speak or name the faces,
and when, new mother, I cut the pills and daily
swallowed those half-moons the way I'd swallow
anything to stop the mind's engine running
till it smoked. In obituaries, the dead are survived
by the living. If I survive you, I'll be haunted
for years, hauling our story up and down stairs,
across dog-clawed oak floors. I'll pull it through
the streets we walked, naming the trees: tulip poplar,
paper birch, pin oak. I'll coil it and heave it into bed
each night. If I'm the last of us, my long white hair
will be so heavy, heavy and thick as rope, I won't cut it.

Far in the Hole

by Jennifer Haigh

Jennifer Haigh's acclaimed novel Heat and Light, *of which this is what she calls an out-take, was published by Ecco Press in May 2016. About the writing that 'never appears in the novel,' Jennifer had this to say:* 'In drafting a novel, I give myself permission to follow every thread of story that fascinates me. This keeps the process interesting, and results in livelier, more surprising books; but as methods go, it's hideously inefficient. Over the course of five novels, I've written hundreds and hundreds of pages that will never be read by anyone.'

Heat and Light looks at what happens to Bakerton, Pennsylvania when the natural gas industry comes to town, how this struggling community is transformed and divided by the sudden promise of wealth. The story is intimately connected to Pennsylvania's unique history as an energy state. The first oil well in the world was drilled there. The Three Mile Island nuclear disaster happened there. Coal companies dominated its economy for a hundred years. Each of these subjects is worthy of several novels, and my early drafts of *Heat and Light* include long digressions about each. Most of those pages didn't make it into the final draft. This scene is from the first draft of *Heat and Light*. The year is 1987, and Lorne Trexler — a geology professor at a small private college and an unreconstructed hippie — is taking his Earth Science class on a field trip to Centralia, a former coal mining town. Readers of *Heat and Light* will recognize both Trexler and his student, Amy Rubin.'

Amy Rubin stared out the window of the bus. "Seriously, this is Centralia? There's nothing *here*."

"Exactly," said Professor Trexler. "That's the whole point."

The bus turned down a side street and parked at a cemetery. In sweatshirts and sunglasses, ponytails and ball caps, the students filed out into the street. Trexler had brought, over the years, a dozen Earth Science classes to Centralia. This group reacted as all the others had. Driving into town, only a few had bothered to look out the window. Now they pissed and moaned about the smell.

The narrow street was lined with boarded-up houses, all alike: shingles and aluminum siding, peeling paint and sagging porches, a look of established poverty. The air smelled of struck matches, a car backfiring. Sometimes it smelled of bicycle tires or rotten eggs. The smell changed day to day, in response to conditions underground. The exact reasons it changed were not known.

There was life here, once. There was uptown and downtown. There was an American Legion post and a VFW, a Roman Catholic church and several bars. Each December the local paper published letters to Santa. High school football was played. They were working people, not rich. They had nothing, they had everything. Parades for the patriotic holidays, the local High Steppers in their spangled costumes, silver batons spinning. The Fire Queen in her sister's old prom dress, waving from the back of someone's convertible. Church festivals in summertime, bingo under striped tents, funnel cakes, nickel games for the kids. There were summer weddings, a rash of them after high school graduation, the church hall decked with Kleenex flowers and bridesmaids dancing barefoot, their high heels lying in a pile near the door.

They were coal miners, miners' wives, and miners' children, until they weren't. The town's heyday came and went. The underground mines were abandoned, and the town limped along with a little strip mining, the traces of which were still present, razed land no one had bothered to backfill, sooty black scars as though the earth had been burned. Centralia contracted but did not disappear. Despite the privations, people found a way to stay. The town budget shrank a little every year. Soon there was no money for July fireworks, for Christmas decorations on Main Street. Trash pickup was a luxury the town couldn't afford. Citizens could pay a hauler to take their trash to the town dump, or carry it there themselves.

The dump ran along the town's western border, a deep, gaping pit dug a generation earlier, one of the first strip mines. By the early 1960s the trash was three stories deep, decades' worth of castoff furniture and old appliances, car parts and dead batteries, paint cans and household waste. Like all of Centralia it sat directly sat on a coal seam, called the Buck Vein, that stretched wishbone-shaped beneath the town.

How the fire began isn't hard to imagine. Every house in Centralia was warmed by a coal-fired Heatrola. An ashcan filled with soot and embers sat at every back door. Along with the usual household trash, the ashcans were emptied at the dump — atop the furniture and appliances, the car parts and batteries. Atop a seam of anthracite coal.

The town officials didn't panic. A fire at the dump wasn't unusual. The volunteer firemen sent a pumper truck to wet the garbage down. When the fire kept burning, they sent a bulldozer to dig through the landfill and expose the fire. The pumper gave the flaming trash a good soaking. Then the firemen went home.

The fire smoldered but did not extinguish. Instead it traveled underground. It would have petered out eventually, suffocated by tons of earth, if it hadn't found its way to the mine.

A mine — open space, a series of empty rooms — has oxygen, necessary for combustion. The old Centralia Colliery mine was an immense man-made furnace, lined with anthracite coal.

Coal burns and burns, endlessly, reliably. This is the entire point of coal.

Underground, the fire raced along the Buck Vein. Aboveground, the people of Centralia noticed a peculiar smell. Rotten eggs, bicycle tires. The fumes drifted across Locust Avenue and into St. Ignatius Church.

For eight weeks fire raced along the coal seam. Finally the borough council notified the state. They were vague about when and how the fire had started. Spontaneous combustion, the state inspector was told.

The fire burned and burned.

Centralia wasn't the first underground fire in Pennsylvania. It was a known hazard of coal mining: *Far in the hole!* The old coal barons had fought such fires aggressively, to protect their investment. They flooded the mines with water, or dug the burning seams clean out of the ground. But the Centralia mine was long abandoned, dug in the last century by a company long bankrupt. It was nobody's problem now.

"The worst part," Trexler told his students, "the real tragedy, is that none of this had to happen. It could have turned out differently." If the town officials had acted quickly, and notified the state Bureau of Mines. If government—local, state and federal—had brought its resources to bear.

He was silent for a moment, long enough to make the students uncomfortable.

"I don't get it," said Amy Rubin. "Why did they wait so long?"

It was, to Trexler, a moment of transcendent beauty: a voice —at last!—ringing with the clarity of youth, its righteous indignation. Youth ought to love nothing better than passing judgment, the invigorating pleasure of moral outrage.

"Good question, Rubin. Why do you think?"

Another silence.

"Here's a hint," said Trexler. "The state had a bunch of regulations for managing landfills. This one was supposed to be covered with clay once a week, something moist and non-flammable."

"So, wait. They could have prevented it, if they just did what they were supposed to do?" said Suki Lee.

Trexler spread his open hands.

"So they were covering their asses," said Scott McKotch, Trexler's favorite burnout, a pot-addled kid who came to class red-eyed and dreamy, when he came at all.

"Yeah, maybe. Definitely. From our current perspective the Borough council acted like sheepish schoolboys. The kid who threw the baseball through the neighbor's window. Of course, there was a deeper reason." Trexler paused. "Some of you are going to fight me on this. What if I told you that they waited because they were poor?"

Snorts from the frat boys: Earth Science, considered a gut course, attracted more than its share. They greeted Trexler's political rants with loud derision. Trip Dingman, a standout on the golf team, began whistling. In the front row, Suki Lee rolled her eyes.

To be nineteen years old and admit, without apparent self-consciousness, a fondness for golf.

The town burned and burned.

"Okay, dig this. In 1962, Centralia's General Fund had two thousand dollars. Two grand to plow the roads all winter, to fill potholes, to clean up the mess when the sewers backed up. They could use that two grand to keep the town running. Or, I guess, spread clay on the garbage dump once a week."

Trip Dingman, smartass, whistled "Blowin' in the Wind."

The rest of the students were silent. Beneath their feet the fire was unstoppable, raging out of control.

The Wedding Toppers

by Richard Garcia

A bride and groom, two figurines, topped a wedding cake. After the wedding photographer had backed into the cake to try to get a better shot of the lucky couple, they never saw the rest of the wedding. The cake and photographer had fallen together. The bride and groom were both well-known poets and each had their own stalker who came to each of their weddings. After the cake fell, one stalker's hand plunged through the cake after the toppers but they escaped into a closet, where they found a large shoe to live in. It was crowded in the shoe and after seven years the landlady asked them to leave. The wedding toppers found a nice cottage in a snow globe to live in. They would stand at the window of the cottage and marvel at the snow. They knew it was not real snow but that was fine with them. The snow fell on the front lawn, on the picket fence. It lay quietly on the mailbox. Not a real mailbox.

Tattoo

by Gregory Lawless

Originally I wanted a tattoo of my tattoo artist
giving me the tattoo itself but he said
"boundaries" and demanded I peruse
the tattoo photographs cascading
down his sheetrock walls. How about a tattoo
of sheetrock? I said, and then he made me
flip through a book of dragons. "Lots of people
get sleeves these days," he added, and I said maybe
the sleeve of a nice blue dress shirt
down the length of my arm…
and so he gave me a book of complicated
knots to consider. "Do you like this one?"
he asked. "It's called the Knot of Destiny."
How bout a frayed knot? I asked, and he just
looked around. I think maybe a tattoo of how
your neck swivels evasively, I said, would make
a nice tattoo. Or a tattoo of one of your
many tattoos. "That would be the tattoo itself," he said,
"iterated across your naïve flesh." I don't think
any of these tattoos are really me, I said,
and he told me that I would become the tattoo
and vice versa. That the tattoo didn't say much
about the person until it was part of the person
at which point it had no choice but to reveal
something, no matter where it is hidden.
I said that sounded interesting, which is exactly
what you say when something

isn't. "Why don't you a get a quote wrongly attributed
to Oscar Wilde put somewhere on your thigh?"
he asked, and I said good question, because
they all are, in my experience, each one better
than the last.

A year later, when I was teaching in Lebanon, I belonged to a gym where there was a belly dance class.

they're all so beautiful & accomplished

Why not come in & try it?

It's fun!

It looks fun!

I'm too shy! They'll all find out how uptight and Anglo I am!

I've got to go!

WIMP!

At a friend's wedding in Beirut, a Tunisian friend of the bride danced astoundingly in a very un— "I dream of Jeanie" costume.

Lalalalala!

And then everyone danced. Wow those Lebanese archaeologist girls could really move. I tried my be—

During the excavation at Troy where I worked the next summer, there was a mandatory dance party in a cafe in the village.

This is not a sit-down party. Now you must dance.

The village girls who worked in the kitchen on the dig needed no encouragement.

Herr Prof. Doktor Korfmann, Chief excavator from Tübingen.

It was amazing to see them danc_ & also to see the boys' eyes pop at th_

The different styles of dance are unified by some basic moves based on muscle isolations —

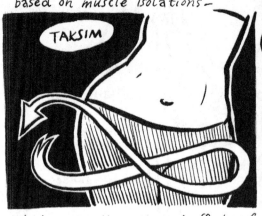

which causes the magical effect of the upper & lower body moving independently —

Emily, show us how to undulate!

and can be combined in response to the music & to other dancers

It's so unlike any other form of dance I've tried (which is not many).

Not a single dosey-doe.

And I've found a community of dancers.

My husband John is very supportive.

Have a great time at your harem class!

Stop calling it that!

Beautiful hand-sewn Egyptian costume he bought me for X-mas.

TO PARADISE, I GIVE MY HALF-FORGOTTEN DREAMS

by Jon Thompson

I

So this is
it. Is it
singular in itself
still, whole, inviolate
despite the many
depredations? You can
see slender branches
waving gently in
the dispensation of
the wind, ignorant
of all but
the essential. The
rustle of lightness
stirs the world.
Though few believe
it, there's no
sin. Unspeakable atrocity
yes; ordinary cruelties,
yes; but no
sin. Even now,
the world's impossibly
verdant & self-possessed.
In the whisperings
of a late autumnal

light, the pure
weight, the inertia,
the opacity of
the past, seems
like a distant
memory no longer
capable of arrowing
you. But that
you will be
arrowed is inescapable.
That's the deal:
beauty holds out
many promises, many
balms, but it will
not save you.

II

Here, of course,
it's only beauty
that can save you.
But salvation does
not come without
cost. Its uncanniness
must be lived,
thrilling, but deeply
uncomfortable, like visiting
a museum with
room after room
open to the sky,
full of streaming
sunlight, in

which paintings of
inexpressible beauty
just by being there
indict a lesser world.
Or when taking
a walk &
seeing –still alive!–
the artless, simple
Painted Trillium,
the simple Star
of Bethlehem, the
yellow & white
Alium, the violet
yellow & white
Dwarf Crested Iris,
testaments to
the flagrant beauty
we live with
without regard for
its delicate, salvational
force. True beauty,
it turns out,
is unendurable. Its
promise is too
painful, too immense
to rise to, the
possibilities too frightening.
It is comforting,
instead, to render
the world ugly,
beyond redemption. Here
paradise is the

unconsciousness, unknowable
but silently
framing what's possible.
How many other
civilizations have
achieved our level
of despoliation, our
unregenerate ugliness?
We've replaced the
real with the
destructiveness
of the ideal.
The need to
forget then triumphs
over the imperative
to change. In
paradise, tragedies cannot
ever be seen.

III

In paradise, wants
& needs become
indistinguishable, making
it the culmination
of generations of
confused desire. Each
desire becomes layered
with new generations of
desire making it
palimpsestic. Therefore, the
culmination of everything

to be feared.
I want, for instance,
not an end
to the tawdry, but
a limit. I want
the feeling of
American vastness to
be accompanied by
intimacy. I want streets
of a new
dawn, not closed-
down glamour avenues
of dusk, the shopfront
displays radiant with
expense. I want
clocks in public
places with hands
that will go
backwards stopping
at moments of
singular possibility,
just to remember
what that is
like. I want
death to not be
a corrupt stranger.
I want cities
in which
art is more
than proof of
baroque wealth. I
want all the old

grand dreams of
the avant-garde
to be as
common & actual
as trash. I
want the ruins we
created honored
with pilgrimages.
I want trash
everywhere
to be luminous.

IV

Paradise means fear.
Fear that someone
will take it
away. Fear that
it was not
what was desired;
fear that it
will not be
what was desired.
Fear that what
is beautiful will
be subtracted from
your life, too.
Fear that it
is as beautiful as
it seems. A
nation can fantasize,
but fear &

desire start with
individuals. And what
you fear, you
can desire &
what you desire,
you'll always fear.
To live in
paradise means
accepting a high
level of vulnerability
as the defining
condition of your
life. To be
vulnerable without ever
being able to
admit it is
to be condemned
to living a
kind of double
life, lived &
passed from generation
to generation, an inescapable
inheritance, unspoken but
expressed in the
language of gesture,
especially in our
fearful violence, which
despite its abject
unboundedness, is always,
among other things,
an unacknowledged plea
for forgiveness.

V

If I could remember
the scene completely
it'd be something
like this: evening,
and being
stuck on a highway
with hundreds of
other cars stopped
in traffic. But
the light, the
light was dazzling,
a glinting that
came from a
thousand reflections
shimmering off
glassfronts, a rejoinder
to the sun, less
the light of
transcendence & more
a reply to
nature, a testament
to what is, what
isn't now
possible, as when
the traffic moved
again, & the
unified shimmering disappeared
& the moment
returned to the
quotidian, the

terror not in
the moment of
a thousand windshields
flickering & glinting,
but in the
banality of the
big-box chain-
stores that lined the
highway with all
the signs
pointing to other
signs, indifferent to
any other transaction.

Provincetown Sketches, Part 1

by Timothy Patrick McCarthy

*B*efore marriage, the gays had some nice things: bars without bachelorette parties, Pride marches without corporate logos, relationships without state recognition *and* straight expectation. We also had some naughty things: bathhouses and glory holes, poppers and polyamory, fabulous faggotry and a fucking sense of humor! These days, I worry that much of this is on the Acela train to extinction, that we are losing our liberation in the assimilation revolution.

At least there's still Provincetown.

The Vault

My husband is not a big talker. That's mostly my job. But he went all in that night—and things got real awkward, real fast.

In retrospect, the dinner was probably set up to be awkward. After our first two days of vacation in Ptown, we met my uncle and his friend at Front Street, their favorite restaurant. That's what we called him—my uncle's "friend"—not because we didn't *know*, but because my Catholic, working-class family has a longstanding "don't ask, don't tell" policy when it comes to those of us who could never seem to find the "right girl" (and for the girls, the "right boy") to marry. Growing up, my uncle and I were never really that close, in part, because I was a bratty, entitled closet queen who resented him for not flaming a trail to make it easier for me when I finally came out in my late twenties. (As if that was *his* burden.) Ever since I moved to Boston for college in the summer of 1989—my uncle lives in the suburbs—my mother has been pressuring me to get closer to her brother. "You two have so much in common," she would say. I always hated hearing that.

This was the first time the four of us had been together without other family members around to prop up the straight charade. And this was Provincetown, where you leave your closet, if you have one, on the ferry. We exchanged hugs, ordered drinks, and buried ourselves in the menu. My vodka martini barely hit the table before I swept it up and gulped a third of it down. I didn't care that it tasted like the ocean.

"So, how did you two meet?" my husband broke the silence.

Are you fucking kidding me? We don't ask these kinds of questions in our family.

"At The Vault," my uncle's friend said. "Have you two ever been?"

The Vault?

"No, where is it?" My husband was curious.

Was he trying to kill me?

Another third of the martini disappeared.

"It's just down Commercial Street. You should go sometime."

Thanks for the recommendation, friend!

"We met at The Vault," my uncle chimed in.

We've established this already. Please just let our friends talk.

"We also spent a lot of time riding on the bike paths."

Oh no. Not the bike paths.

My uncle looked at his friend with that kind of knowing smile that betrays a good metaphor: "He used to be a real slut!"

Not that. Not this. Not here. Not in front of us.

"Speak for yourself!" his friend shot back, both of them snorting loudly.

I ordered another martini.

The initial awkwardness did not result in the Armageddon I had anticipated. Quite the contrary, we had a lovely meal. My husband and I eventually shared our own bar and "bike riding" stories from the slutty years. Along the way, we learned that the two of them had been more than "friends" since the early nineties, dating back to my college years, when mom first urged me to reach out to her brother. Turns out they had been coming to Ptown for most of that time, had a place here. In other words, they had a *history*. They told story after story, shared a dessert, laughed at each other's jokes, touched each other's hands, and ribbed each other like those old couples sometimes do after a lifetime of everything. It was the happiest I had ever seen my uncle. His boyfriend—or partner, still not sure how they refer to each other—clearly brought out the best in him. They both seemed *free*. After dinner, we said our goodbyes, and my husband and I agreed that we want to be more like them when we grow up.

But we also had something else on our mind: *The Vault.*

I fired up Google on my iPhone: 247 Commercial Street. After running into two friends, who had just purchased new sex toys at Eros, and Tony Kushner, who was walking his dog—this is Ptown, after all—I turned to my husband: "We're going." He smiled, because he knew that not even my favorite living playwright could deter us from our destination.

There is perhaps nothing more pathetic than being the first two people in the leather bar just after it opens. Turns out "The

Vault" is aptly named. The only light in the place comes from the small television sets showing filthy porn from a time when men used neither clippers nor condoms, and the bar-length string of red Christmas lights that illuminate the oversized dildos and assorted butt plugs that hang along the wall above the liquor. It's hard to know how big The Vault actually is when you first step foot in the place, since the nether regions beyond the ends of the bar are terrifyingly, tantalizingly dark.

"Early bird special, boys?" the muscled, mustached bartender came to us. He looked like a vestige from a vintage era (circa the porn on the television sets). We must have reeked like rookies.

We ordered a Maker's, neat, and a vodka soda. (Should have skipped the soda, because the bartender mostly did.) My husband nodded his head in the direction of an imposing wooden structure that looked like the early 20th century electric chairs I had seen in history books in graduate school. It was near the wall next to the bathroom. Or was that the entrance to a dungeon? Hard to tell. I squinted to get a better look. The chair had no proper seat; instead, there was a large orange pylon whose top six or seven inches protruded upwards, beyond the horizon of where one's ass might sit, should one choose to rest it there. On either side, there were poles with what looked like adjustable wrist-sized straps. I couldn't decide if all of this was hot or horrifying.

"Is that what I think it is?" I asked my husband.

He smiled and turned his attention to the bareback gang-bang on TV.

"First time here?" The bartender placed the two drinks down in front of us, and leaned in.

"Actually, yes!" Then I proceeded to unleash the world's longest run-on sentence about how we had come to pay our respects (wrong phrase, I know) to my uncle who used to come here (maybe still does?) with his friend (oops, I mean partner) and they met here back in the day and they have a place in Ptown so this is my husband and we're here on vacation from Boston for the first time and we got married last year but we're definitely not boring and we decided we wanted to see where it all started for them and also The Vault sounded cool and we know it's early but we were in the neighborhood for dinner down the street and we're always up for something new and blah etcetera yeah fuck stop talking.

My husband looked at me as he often does. So I shut up.

"Are they dead?"

The bartender looked confused.

"Oh, no! We aren't 'paying our respects' like *that*. They're still alive. Very healthy! We just wanted to visit the place where they first met. We just found out they were more than 'friends.' Well, not really, but…we just had dinner at Front Street. Delicious! They went home, but we…they said we'd like it here."

That look again.

"Oh, they're just *old*," the bartender's laugh came as a collective relief. "Well, welcome to The Vault, where fantasies really do come true! That'll be eighteen dollars, gentlemen." He winked, slapped our twenty on the bar, and shoved it inside the drawer of the old cash register, the kind that sings when it's stimulated.

We didn't stay long enough to indulge any fantasies. Between the pylon throne, the old-school porn, and the dildo-butt plug holiday decorations, my ass was starting to get a little nervous. And other folks—mostly bears and daddies—were starting to arrive, looking at us as if they smelled rookie, too. We sucked down our drinks and slapped a couple more bucks on the bar. I knew we'd be back, though. My husband and I like a little dark and dirty from time to time.

For whatever the reason, as we were leaving The Vault, I felt a peculiar urge to call my mother and tell her all about our evening. Over-sharing is something of a vocation for me.

"Mom, we had a great time at dinner! They told us all about their life together! Did you know they've been together since the early 1990s? Did you know they met at a leather bar in Province-town? It's called The Vault!"

My husband just shook his head. He married a hopeless man.

"That's great, honey. I'm so glad you and your uncle are spending more time together."

I didn't tell her about the pylon or the porn. It would have been too much.

Tea Dance

"Tea Dance" takes place outside, in broad daylight, with boys and booze as far as the eye can see. As long as the weath-er is good—and in the summer months, even when it isn't—Tea Dance is on, 4-7 p.m. daily, at the Boatslip Resort. "Resort" might be something of an overstatement, unless it means that if every other place in Provincetown is booked, you may have to resort to staying here. Still, I love the double entendre. The gays are famous for this. We really are witty.

I discovered "Tea" during my first trip to Ptown many years ago—before I got gay married but after I got old and fat—and I've been coming ever since. I'll admit, as a middle-aged academic who is also a former college athlete, I am sometimes susceptible to the worst of our prejudices about age (the younger the better) and body type (the fitter the better). Whenever I enter a gay space—es-pecially one dominated by gay men—I worry about whether I'm too fat, too old, and/or too ugly to be there. (Years ago, one of my favorite queens tried to comfort me by saying, "Yeah, but it must feel good to be so smart," which offered little consolation.) I am not proud of this, of course. But it does help to explain why I always try to surround myself in such venues with loved ones—straight friends, my lesbian sisters, other queer folks like me, people who won't judge—to serve as an antidote to the chronic self-loathing that sometimes threatens to tear me apart even when I should be having fun. Even when I have every right, as we all do, to be as fucking fierce and free as any person alive. Herein lies my love-hate relationship with things like Tea Dance. I guess I'm a glutton for punishment.

That day, I did the unthinkable: I went to Tea *alone*. What's worse, I arrived early. I planned to meet some folks there, but they were running late. *Party of one, your place by the railing near the outdoor bar is ready.*

As my friends know, I am *never* early. So when my hand was stamped by the bouncer at 4:15 p.m., as I walked out onto the nearly empty Boatslip deck, I decided to go to the bathroom—mostly, to bide a bit of time and do one more mirror check before things got crowded.

In Tea terms, "fashionably late" has little to do with fashion, per se, because fashion usually requires clothing, which is often in short supply during Tea. Ever since the bulges in my arms and chest and legs migrated to my belly, I've had to be very careful about what to wear, especially during the summer: busy shirts that absorb the sweat without showing it, baggy shorts that are more the former than the latter, colorful sneakers that might distract attention, cool accessories that might start a conversation. It all sounds so pathetic (especially now that I'm writing it down) but at least I know I'm not alone. The struggle is real, people.

Evidently, shit was also getting real in the Boatslip bathroom at 4:15 p.m., where I encountered two young men huddled against one another. They both looked vaguely like Justin Bieber. At first, I thought they might be kissing, which would have been sweet enough, or jerking each other off, which seemed unnecessarily premature given the hour.

"Hey, daddy, do you mind if we do a little coke?"

Daddy? Damn. Not helping.

"Far be it from me to breakup a bathroom bump," I said with every ounce of alliterative intention (and "Sex and the City" realness) I could muster. I figured: *If I have to be a Daddy, goddammit, I'm gonna be the cool Daddy.*

As I pretended to pee, I heard them snickering, then a few short sniffs, then silence. Finally the bathroom mirror was all mine. I sucked my stomach in and stuck my chin out, pulled my shirt away from the waistline in the hopes that it would stay there, and then walked with over-compensating confidence out onto the still mostly empty deck. I ordered the signature Boatslip rum drink and took my place, alone, by the railing near the outdoor bar.

By the time my friend got there, I was two rum drinks in. They call it "Planter's Punch," and I often wonder if "plant" refers to *face plant*, as in: "if you drink too many of these during Tea, you are likely to do a face plant before you get to Spiritus Pizza." (I've seen more than a few queens meet their demise this way over the years.)

My friend was actually a former student. He was clearly in his element—a charismatic 20-something with just the right mix of smarts and sass to be a big hit in these parts. Truth is, I both admired and envied him, so out and proud at such an early age, with the whole world ahead of him. I suppose he felt similarly about me, given that I had survived the world so far and seemed to be flourishing despite it all. Such is the dynamic, sometimes, between queer professors and queer students—looking backward and forward from the same present, lugging different baggage around in a difficult world that still demands solidarity. I hugged him.

I also bought him a Planter's Punch of his own as he introduced me to the friends he brought with him: a roommate about his age, and two older men who were probably mine. His roommate, unusually energetic from "pre-gaming," asked me why I wasn't "mixing and mingling."

Without thinking, I said what I always say when random folks approach me at my perch on the margins of a gay club: "Because I'm a Gore Vidal-in-training—aloof and cranky, yet fabulous and well worth the effort." My student, God bless him, laughed loudly, as did the two men-of-a-certain-age. Blank stares from the room-mate, though, who had no idea what I was talking about and defi-nitely needed a good lesson in gay history and Gore Vidal.

After several more rum punches, we were all having a lovely time, soaking in the warm June sun, swaying to the loud pop mu-sic, talking politics—which in gay circles usually amounted to a coronation of President Obama—and throwing some shade at the drunk twink who better watch himself tonight and the grown-ass queens who should've known better than to wear those tiny lime green thongs and not a damn thing else. (So much for not judging!)

The thing about the rum punch is that you have to pee more than usual. Half hoping I would run into my bathroom bump bud-dies again, I found myself at the back of a very long line for the loo. When I finally got to the urinal, as if choreographed, Cher's "Believe" started playing, and I overheard the following exchange:

Young Gay #1: "Cher is playing."

Young Gay #2: "I thought she was dead."

Young Gay #3: "I think she's still alive. She Tweeted some-thing yesterday."

Feeling fabulous and free, I shouted: "Cher will never die!"

As I turned, an older gay man—older than me—raised his hand in solidarity, gave me a high five, and shouted back: "That's the best conversation I've heard all day!"

When I returned to the deck, the vibe had shifted. I sudden-ly realized that the four folks I was hanging out with were, well, something of a foursome. One of the older gentlemen leaned in and whispered to me that he had recently met my former student online. The other older gentleman—like me, a college professor—had his hand firmly attached to the roommate's waist. I was definitely the fifth wheel.

You know what, good for them. But it was clearly time for this professor to grab a single slice at Spiritus and go the hell home.

Dick Dock

I learned about the "Dick Dock" in a T-shirt store during my first trip to Ptown many years ago. I knew what "dick docking" was, of course, but I suspected this particular tank top—the color of original Gatorade with big black letters—was referring to something altogether different. So I asked the cashier a rookie question: where is it?

Turns out, the Dick Dock is located right *under* the Tea Dance deck at the Boatslip. Convenient, I thought: top by day, bottom by night. Made perfect sense.

For those who don't know, Dick Dock is Provincetown's version of the myriad public spaces across the United States—parks and truck stops, bathrooms and back alleys, libraries and locker rooms—where gay men and other folks (some queer, some trans, some closeted or "discreet") go to fuck around. I've been to more than a few in my lifetime—the Rambles in New York City, the Fens in Boston, other places I can no longer name—usually late at night, but not always. (One of the best blowjobs I ever got was from an Irish guy on a Sunday morning when both of us should have been at Mass.) These are not safe spaces, in the strictest sense. They are heavily policed, increasingly so over the years, and prone to some dangerous behavior. There is sometimes violence and other criminal activity. People have been beaten and murdered there. But they are also places that promise some degree of sexual freedom, delivered in the dual form of anonymity and promiscuity. Even the occasional politician or celebrity risks power and privilege to visit them every now and then, and one can hardly blame them (unless they are anti-gay Republicans, in which case you should always blog about it). For those of us who are more ordinary—and this was especially true before the Internet—these are places to release sexual tension, find social connection, even make some money in a world that often stigmatizes us for doing any of these things on our own terms.

During an early trip to Ptown, I decided I would visit the Dick Dock. Not to have sex, necessarily, but to check out the scene. I know this must sound ridiculous—and perhaps it's a lame justification for what didn't take place—but it's true: that night, I was more curious than horny. Still, I've always maintained that if you're new to town—even in Ptown—you should make every effort to get to know the lay of the land (so to speak). And that meant getting to the bottom of Tea Dance, after dark.

Following last call at Crown and Anchor, I walked, heart racing, chain smoking, down Commercial Street to the alley on the west side of the Boatslip. I didn't really know where I was going, but I figured if I ended up in the ocean, I had gone too far. The nearly full moon was reflecting hard on the water. It was brighter than I expected, or wanted. I tried not to get distracted by the terrible beauty of it all. And I kept my head down hoping that the lowered rim of my Yankees hat would hide my nervous eyes. Just before I reached the water's edge, feet sinking into the shoreline, I began to hear the familiar sounds—the unmistakable grunts and groans, slurping, sucking, stroking—that I had heard in Central Park and the Fenway, and in the other places, usually cities, I had visited. I turned left and made my peace with the sand in my sneakers.

The first thing I saw was a dick. Pretty good dick, actually: thick, pink, good head, getting hard in his hand. He reached to see mine. I waved him off without speaking, like some kind of gay

Obi-Wan Kenobi: *this isn't the dick you're looking for.* On any given night, I might have sucked or jerked him off—or asked for the same. But honestly, as I was getting older, I was also getting smarter (if that's what you call it) about whipping my dick out in public. And that night, I had promised myself that I was there only in my role as cultural anthropologist—the Margaret Mead of mutual masturbation.

(Speaking of smart, I can't help but contemplate how much has changed in the age of smartphones. When I first started having public sex in my mid-twenties, we didn't have the luxury of the treacherous technological threesome of cell phones with built-in camera and internet. Hell, we barely had cell phones or internet! Back in the day, if you wanted to have sex with a stranger, you either had to call someone and have phone sex, chat with someone on your home computer and then arrange a time and place to meet, or roam around the park and hope for the best. Clearly I'm no prude—and I'm certainly not at all interested in policing anyone else's behavior or good time—but damn if smartphones don't freak me out when it comes to fucking. Nowadays, I feel like you really do have to be smarter about whipping your dick out—or just not give a fuck—lest you find yourself in a Facebook Live porn shoot accompanied by Instagram stills and Snapchat play-by-play. It's enough to make you want to stay home, fire up RedTube, and jerk off like old school. But I digress.)

The scene that night could only have happened during lower tide. Dozens of men, perhaps a hundred or so total, strewn all along the underbelly of the deck: some in larger groups doing their thing; some in pairs or threesomes getting it on; some alone, still— or just—looking. Among the latter, I walked along the shoreline, trying my best to avoid eye contact, taking it all in but talking to no one. The things that struck me about the Dick Dock are the same things that always strike me about spaces like this: it was the most diverse group of people—in terms of age, race, ethnicity, class, body type, everything but gender—that I had seen in any one place all day; many of us had seen each other at various bars and clubs earlier in the night, which didn't seem to faze anyone; no one appeared to want anything more, in terms of a "relationship," than what they were getting in that moment; and the sex was both ample and consensual. On that night, at least, the Dick Dock seemed like a genuinely safe space, protected and un-policed, a local myth I accepted without question until I heard that a dead man's body washed up on that very shore several years after my visit.

As I walked east to the opposite end of the Dick Dock, away from the masses of men, a cute young guy approached me—broad chest, short hair, tall as me, cautious smile, the kind of man I might have invited home if I were in a different mood and place.

"Where you going?" He was a smoker, too.

Then he grabbed my crotch through my shorts. I hesitated, but it felt good. I closed my eyes and leaned into him. He kept his hand there for a minute or two, rubbing, until I started to get hard. I was about to return the favor, but when his warm breath touched my neck, I pulled away. I looked right at him, almost smiled, and fumbled for my cigarettes.

"Need to go, man. Good luck."

I meant it. Because sometimes, when you're lonely, you go home alone.

Explosion Rocks Springfield

by Rodrigo Toscano

*The Friday evening gas explosion in Springfield leveled a strip club
next to a day care.*
I remember the breeze right before...
Burst of—was it willow—slant-falling.
The gray sidewalk, schist granules, scattering.
A brown dumpster lid smushing its green plastic, sandwich meat.
A rat made its debut, but for a moment.

I remember an awning string's knotted tip soft-thudding a win-
dowpane
—tympani's uneven beat.
The rustle of stray trash—bass strings, almost rising
—but never.
And the chopper, the chopper—spittletatootling, spittletatoo-
tling—
A proud boot landing on obedient asphalt.
The stern, uncrying chrome.
The flighty flames decorative gas tank.

I can't forget the beryllium blue sunshades
—orange hued at a glance.
And the stars and bars, starched, pressed, bandana.
Nation Idol Gorge
But for a moment
Then
Boom.

The Friday evening gas explosion in Springfield leveled a strip club
    next to a day care.
Spartacus sprinklers (top rail)
Serial no. 21809A
Inspector 480F
Jiangxi Quality Products
Night Hawk Importers, San Bruno, CA
Roman Roads Distributors, Phoenix, AZ
Port of entry, Tacoma, WA
Tankard 10179.03
Inspector 4201
ILO quarterly report:
Case study 1142
Tingting Liu, 23, female
I.D. 41732
Platform 12, line 8, station 4
Muscular skeletal paralysis
3rd metatarsal taped to 2nd   phalangeal
4th proximal splinted to 5th distal
OSHA Region 1 final report:
Incident 2267, explosion (gas)
Inspector 505F
Sprinklers inoperable

Logic Tree branch 20
System of Safety failure
Mitigation device
16 drill holes stoppered
Weld burs not filed
Citation: 29CFR.1910.159(c)(12)
Notes: inspector 505F on leave
DOL budget sequestered
PUB.L. 112-25
District 2, 112th Congress
United States of America

The Friday evening gas explosion in Springfield leveled a strip club
     next to a day care.
I remember the plume right after…
Orbs of—was it cinnamon—black-rising.
Vapor gray whitening shingle powder rain.
A dumpster lid sheered off a gravestone's angel face.
A hawk's claws claimed the stump.

I remember two spouts of thin flame, blue, making an X
—mind's waking dream.
The hissing of gurgling plastic, supplicant—sick
—stomach's inner eyeball.
And the bathtub, the bathtub—sittin' pretty—sittin' pretty—
The hysteric roof flopping on an unfazed floor.
The wise, ever-wakeful steel beams.
The cheery glass—beaming—everywhere.

I can't forget that purple doorknob
—horny at a glance.

And the plump couch stuffing foam, blazing, angry.
City's Final Chorus
But for a moment
Then
Shsh.

The Friday evening gas explosion in Springfield leveled a strip club
next to a day care.
Spartacus Sprinklers (top rail)
Serial no. 21809A
Scrap metal yard F-2
Stripped steel tankard 28
Sampson Recyclers Ltd., Pittsfield, MA
Steelworkers local 4-12026
Smelting furnace 48
Slab beam rollout batch 81.2014
Semper Fortis Steel Precision Corp, Brooklyn, NY
Steelworkers local 4-200
Section cutting station no. 12
Steel cylinder hollow type 2b
Store & send department 4
Spirit of 76 Commercial Furnishing Corp, Slidell, LA
Steelworkers local 3-275
Sargon Sprinklers (bottom rail)
Serial no. 321911B
Sink coating station 12
Sanding unit 25
Seal testing station no. 7
Sprinklers standard specification 29CFR1910.159(b)
Station inspector 13
Sales packaging room H

Sort and storage garage 4
Second incidence of forklift crushing worker's toes
Spirit of 76 Personnel Motivation Free Cupcake Fridays director,
    Chet Baker
Steelworkers local 3-275 chief steward, Marynella Fernandez
Section 5, clause 2 "Management shall comply with all state and
    federal standards"
Safety committee grievance no. 78: unannounced station rotations
    / inadequate training
Staff training regulation arbitration hearing 501.P.36
Sargon Sprinklers 1st annual wet t-shirt contest
Super Sonic Dance Club, 3rd Floor, Picayune, MS

*The Friday evening gas explosion in Springfield leveled a strip club
    next to a day care.*
I don't remember the very moment...
Flashes of—was I daydreaming—Biloxi Bound.
The termite swarm at dusk, balling up, sprinkling.
A skeeter swirling in its hotel pool—for the first time.
A no-see-um bug popped out from nowhere—but for a moment—
    to romp.

I can't say I recall Cleopatra's hairpiece flying off in a speeding
    four-cylinder vehicle
—Empire of the Great Somewhere, but never.
And the flying fish, the flying fish—hither-flopping, hither-flop-
    ping—
The carefree palms, twerking, injured.
The bald, unyielding sun, giddy.
Tentative feet in knee high water, gripping.

Have I forgotten the name of that triple IPA—something like
—*Rondez The Moon à la Batshit.*
And the ample sized black pockadots—in my eyes, twerking, care-
    fully.
Empire of the Great Somewhere
But for a moment
Then
Then

Dying Lessons

by Carroll Sandel

1.

My mother sat in the entrance hall of her assisted living residence when I arrived. Her Barbara Bush white hair was brushed neatly, her gnarled toes overlapped in the Clarks sandals she had settled on after returning countless pairs of shoes that hurt her feet. She smiled and said, "You'll never guess who I got a belated ninetieth birthday card from. Jan Carmichael. Forty years later and she still carries the torch for your brother." I steered her wheelchair into the dining room. As I sat beside her, she made no effort to raise her fork. I began to feed her as I had my babies, a mother bird waiting for her to open wide so I could place the food in her mouth.

"You're really pushing those carrots, aren't you?" she said.

After she'd eaten half the meal, we went up to her room and chatted for awhile. "You should go home to your husband, dear." she said, "Take me back downstairs; it's too early for me to turn in." After settling her beside the grand piano in the living room, I bent to kiss her cheek. Then I walked into the entry hall and through the wood door with the smoke glass window.

The phone rang the following morning. "Your mother's eyes are open, but she's not responding," the nurse said. I raced to her residence. The white emergency van with the gold bubble on top waited in the circular drive. In her room, my mother lay on her side, gazing at nothing in particular. "Hi, Mom," I said. "It's Carroll." Her eyes did not move. As the two attendants prepared to lift her onto the stretcher, I thought about those unfocused eyes. Dark chocolate irises that had flickered with amusement when she'd told my teenage daughter, "If you don't like my peaches, don't shake my tree." Those eyes, I remembered. Her dead eyes on the psych ward I had forgotten.

2.

In 1937, Italian neuropsychiatrist Ugo Cerletti developed the idea that using electricity to shock a person might aid in the treatment of severe schizophrenia. He had noted that when pigs were given a shock before being butchered, it anesthetized them. Once Cerletti began human trials, he discovered that after 10 to 20 treatments of placing two electrodes or paddles on a person's forehead, depressed patients had much improved. Early electroconvulsive therapy (ECT) caused such violent convulsions patients sometimes broke bones or fractured their spines. Electronics technology advanced. The primary adverse effects of ECT, confusion and memory loss, remained. Former patients and psychiatrists criticized shock therapy as a brutal way to control mental patients. Until more effective drugs became available in the late 1960s, it continued to be widely used in hospitals throughout the United States.

3.

In the summer of 1964, my mother received her first shock

treatment when hospitalized for depression at Western Pennsylvania Psychiatric Hospital. Her every-other-day ECT continued for six weeks. Following discharge, she could not remember the name of my then teenage sister or on which road she lived. In a few months, her memory returned.

While in social work graduate school two years later, I traveled home for Easter break. My mother's room at Western Psych returns to me now as if it were a dream. She sits in a gray Johnny. Her beauty shop permed hair lies matted and flat against her head. From the beige pleather chair, she stares with eyes dull as her faded Johnny. The previous summer I had been engaged to a young man with curly blonde hair and a lopsided smile. During a visit home, my mother had cornered me and warned, "You don't have to marry the first man who asks you." I now sit on a dark wood chair opposite her, no longer engaged to the blonde man, struggling to write my thesis. In my memory, I don't remember us speaking of those things.

Yet the hospital room can reappear. When I allow the fuzzy recollection of the visit, I envision my mother's eyes, open, but not seeing. Like the black discs in the kitsch paintings of waifs marketed by Walter Keane in the 1950s, her dead eyes dominate her face.

4.

While in college, I decided women either became like their mothers or they turned themselves into their opposites. I had watched my mother give her power away before I was old enough for school. On Election Day, she'd ask my father, "Dave, who are we voting for?" I thought she was silly she couldn't decide that on her own. She did not raise a fuss when my father bought a farm without telling her. He planted a half-acre garden and expected her to can and freeze vegetables all summer long. My mother would threaten on occasion, "Someday we'll drag up already canned jars from the cellar and line them up on the kitchen counter. The old boy won't be able to tell the difference." I knew that wouldn't happen. My mother never stood up for herself.

Following my father's dictum that "A penny saved is a penny earned," I tracked my dollars, unlike my mother who never looked at a price tag or wrote her check transactions in the register. I challenged my Bible School teacher when she did not count the Apocrypha, the collection of ancient texts found in sections between the Old and New Testaments, in her number of books in the Bible. I was responsible; I made sure I was heard. I would not be like my mother.

5.

Fifty years after my mother's first hospitalization and fourteen years after her death, I Googled electroshock therapy. I was ready to understand more about her ECT treatments. On my screen, a small wooden box emerged, perhaps fifteen inches square. It contained gears, bolts and other black paraphernalia. A white cord stuck out one side and was attached to a headset with two white disks.

If I had envisioned how a psychiatrist administered my mother's shock therapy, I would have guessed with a contraption large, menacing, similar to encasing a body in a Magnetic Resonance Image machine. The photograph of this puny ECT box troubled me: Was this the machine that zapped my mother? I typed "electroconvulsive therapy modern machine." Up popped a white metal box. A circular dial was situated on a periwinkle blue panel to the left on the front, a round plug like the connection to my laptop jutted out of the right. The machine resembled a kid's record player capable of spinning 45 rpm vinyls.

In front of my computer, I imagined my way into my mother's experience. What did she feel when the attendants arrived to escort her to her first shock treatment? Had anyone explained what was going to happen? Were her thoughts so disordered from the depression that she could not process where the attendants were taking her? I see my five-foot-two-inch, hundred and twenty-five pound mother, lifted onto a hard table in perhaps an operating theater or maybe in a small colorless room.

Because the word "mild' is used in conjunction with the relaxant administered, I deduce that she was awake when she heard a masked nurse order her, "Open your mouth." A hard guard now gripped her teeth, perhaps making it difficult to swallow the spit collecting in her cheeks. She must have felt sharp tightness when the nurses fastened restraints around her wrists and ankles.

In other articles during my Google search, I learned that the brief infusion of electricity that causes the generalized seizure erases any recall of the shock treatment. The recipients wake confused and unsure where they are. Former patients write about feeling as though chunks of their lives have disappeared. What ran through my mother's mind when she awoke in a foreign room? If she had no memory of a treatment, had her alarm been the same after each shock treatment? My chest heaved, my breathing wheezed through my nostrils as I sat and conjured her eyes when she regained consciousness, fearful as the cow's on the farm I had seen laboring to deliver a breached calf.

6.

After several hospitalizations, doctors diagnosed my mother manic-depressive as she had two hypomanic episodes when she talked too fast, slept too little and had the energy of a whirling dervish. Mostly my mother descended into immobilizing depressions where she wrung her hands until raspberry red, drank Lord Calvert whiskey until she passed out. Then back to the hospital where she was re-shocked.

Once she developed bipolar disorder, the thought that my mother's mental illness genes might lurk within me must have been terrifying. But since we were so different, I suppressed that fear. My mind stalled like brown on a fallen oak leaf before I could explore what those shock treatments meant to my mother, what they might have meant to me.

Living in New England, I avoided seeing her when she was again hospitalized. During my infrequent visits home, her demeanor was flat, without a spark of life. She no longer felt like a mother to me, rather a pathetic person I needed to tolerate. My mother's in-and-out-of-the-hospital routine continued for nine years. Then the unexpected intervened.

7.

Australian psychiatrist John Cade discovered the use of lithium salts to treat mania in 1949. While attempting to isolate a metabolic compound that might be useful in treating the symptoms of schizophrenics, he used lithium urate in rats and found it tranquilized them. Soon Cade was prescribing lithium salts to people and succeeded in controlling mania in chronically hospitalized patients. The rest of the world was slow to adopt this treatment as deaths had occurred from relatively small overdoses. As researchers in Denmark and the United States confirmed lithium's effect on stabilizing mania and depression swings, resistance to its use slowly fell away. The U.S. FDA approved the application of lithium to treat mental illness in 1970.

8.

In 1973, my mother sat in a crushed velvet blue chair in my Cambridge home when she visited my husband, toddler daughter and me. "My doctor is going to prescribe a different medicine for me," she said. "It's new and not many people have used it."

I wish I had believed she would no longer careen through her depressions and her marginally stable periods. But I dismissed the idea that some psychiatrist my mother had found would make that much difference in her life. Yet when I recall our conversation, I hear the eagerness in her voice, remember her face uncharacteristically pearl pink and her eyes glowing as if lit by a candle.

Lithium saved her. My mother's periods of depression disappeared. She borrowed books from the library, babysat grandchildren, lunched with her friends and volunteered at The Cancer Society. She seemed to forget about the shock treatments and what those debilitating periods were like for her, as though her car had no rear view mirror. For several years I kept expecting to hear she was again in the hospital. But in time I began to think of her as the mother I knew before she was diagnosed manic-depressive. I, too, erased my memories of her ECT.

9.

Ten years later, my mother's neat, print-like handwriting turned wiggly, her gait became uneven. Diagnosing Parkinson's disease, a degenerative disorder of the central nervous system, a neurologist added Synthroid and Sinemet to the lithium from her psychiatrist and to pills prescribed by other doctors treating her blood pressure, her heart irregularity. The medications did not interact well. My mother gashed her head against the door frame when she went to the bathroom in the night. She shorted out the phone when she spilled water on it as she lurched through her apartment where she lived.

She was about to turn seventy-seven when my brother who lived near her called. "I'm drowning here. I need some help," he said. My mother's falls had increased, her weekly pill organizer was dotted with missed dosages and she often seemed confused. After I flew to Pittsburgh, I took charge; I got her hospitalized and explored resources nearby, then decided to look for a place near me. I found a retirement home with nursing support five minutes from my house.

At her first doctor's appointment after her move, my mother sat with her hands clasped on her lap. The physician asked what she wanted most. She said, "I'd like to take fewer pills." The doctor lined up her arsenal of medications on his desk. With one swipe, he dumped more than half the bottles into the trash can. A woman emerged who spoke more clearly, shook less and rarely fell.

Surrounded by caretakers, without needing to cook a meal or keep track of her meds, my mother came into her own. Her sense of humor won over the nursing aides, the kitchen help, the desk clerks. She prepared for her doctor's appointments as though they were dates, rehearsing entertaining things she might say. When she was eighty, she was telling her podiatrist a joke when he detected a vascular blockage in her leg. She asked what would happen if she did nothing. The podiatrist showed her tiny spots of gangrene on her toes and said she would lose a leg.

I drove her to Boston for her surgery, her medical chart noting DNR in bold red letters on her lap. As she was functioning so well, I said, "Mom, are you sure about this Do Not Resuscitate order?"

"I'm not in a hurry to go, but when I go, I want to go in a hurry," she said, a quip she repeated often in the following ten years. In 1990, before living wills and advance directives were common, my mother had her plan.

At age eighty-five, an aortic root dissection ripped her heart; her prognosis was dire. I rushed to her hospital room. She smiled and said, "I have been lying here planning the music for my funeral." After several touch-and-go months, my mother returned to her assisted-living apartment.

With the progression of the Parkinson's, her falls became more frequent. The ambulance took her to the community hospital to be examined. As I pushed back the curtain in the ER, she'd say "Carroll, remember, no extreme measures."

"Mom, you're just here to be checked out," I'd reply. "You're fine. I won't forget."

Then a month before the phone call telling me she was not responsive, the nursing director at her residence determined my mother, no longer able to dress herself or push her walker to the dining room, needed to transfer to a room with three other women in the nursing home section. My sister and I moved her to an assisted-living facility nearby where she could live in her own room with added support.

Unable to follow my mother at her new residence, her physician wrote to those responsible for her care. He described her very strong beliefs about resuscitation. She had always refused Pneumovax believing that pneumonia was the old woman's friend and had turned down blood transfusions when she had a bleeding ulcer from gastritis. When I read the physician's letter, I marveled at this woman who had refused medical options.

Three weeks after she turned ninety, I received the nurse's phone call. My mother had suffered a stroke. Once she was settled in her hospital room, her eyes flashed anxiety when roaming the room and landing on my sister and me. She garbled sounds indicating she was desperate to tell us something, but she could not process what anyone was asking her. The following day she lay unconscious. The doctor explained her brain might be swelling and offered the comfort care option. An IV would administer morphine for pain, but fluids would be minimal. Over the course of a day or two, my mother's kidneys would shut down, a painless way for her to die.

I wished I'd had a fire drill or two to prepare me for how to handle this dilemma. What was my mother trying to tell us? Was she saying, "Fix me. Don't let me die"? I needed to tell the doctor what we wanted to do. Then, as if hands had grabbed my shoulders, I shook myself. "I am not in a hurry to go, but when I go, I want to go in a hurry." My mother had given me a gift. I dared not refuse it.

Throughout the next day we sat beside where she lay, eyes closed. An IV dripped morphine into her arm. Around four o'clock in the afternoon, my mother's eyes opened, but she stared beyond us. Her brown irises looked blacker, close to matching her pupils. Gone was the hint of a laugh, gone the deadness of depression. At six-thirty, as sunlight filtered through the shades, my mother shut her eyes for the final time.

10.

As I have moved into my Medicare years, I begin to think about dying. I have had few health problems, each resolved quickly. Yet physical issues may crop up at anytime, I know. Do I have the strength my mother did to face what lies ahead?

I think about the years she fought depression. In 1971, not long after I'd had my first baby, my mother turned over the photographs of her grandchildren on the fireplace mantel and swallowed all her pills. She was barely breathing when she arrived at the hospital. Once alert, she said, "I couldn't face another day." Death did not frighten her. She had been up close to it before.

I question now: did her ECT treatments and her mental disorder fortify my mother? Much of the time during those nine years, she appeared affectless, at the mercy of spiraling depressions. Was she marshaling forces I did not detect? After lithium stabilized her, she coped with Parkinson's which robbed her of easy mobility. Her "go along to get along" attitude served her well as she adapted to and survived each health crisis. Yet in her later years, she seemed determined to work the hand she was dealt.

How did she become so clear about when she wanted to die?

I imagine her observing Dorothy who dressed in flared skirts like Loretta Young and played Gershwin tunes on the piano in the carpeted living room until she began accusing the aides of stealing her jewelry and disappeared to the nursing home section. She recounted how her friend, Marian, suffering from chronic diarrhea and no longer able to digest food, told her, "It's time to go." Admiration lingered in my mother's voice. Then the nursing director at her residence said she needed more care and my mother moved to the new facility. She was dead in less than a month. She knew her exit cue.

11.

In 2013, Katy Butler wrote *Knocking on Heaven's Door*, a memoir about her experience with doctors who refused to remove a pacemaker from her father who was severely disabled from a stroke and dementia. The father had been a brilliant college professor but had suffered a stroke when he was seventy-nine. Though he had recovered some functioning, his speech and mental acuity were quite compromised. Doctors suggested a year later that he needed a pacemaker to stabilize his heart, but no one explained that the pacemaker would keep his heart strong while his dementia increased. Several years later as his condition worsened, Katy and her mother asked that the pacemaker be removed, but doctors refused. When Katy's mother developed serious health problems after her husband's death, she made different choices and despite doctors offering more medical treatment, she declined. In Dr. Atul Gawande's book, *Being Mortal*, he described a different path he and his father together chose as his father's health was failing: to prioritize what was most important to him as the end of his life grew closer.

12.

My mother rallied after blocked artery surgery and her aortic dissection, but she had not pursued measures that might interfere with nature taking its course. She had refused blood transfusions, never agreed to pneumonia shots. She knew death would come to us all. By not fighting the inevitable, she let go and went in a hurry.

I look to my mother to learn her lessons. If I imagine myself in her shoes—undergoing ECT, periods of dreading each new day, years of maneuvering her walker—I feel her determination as never before. When she was slightly older than I am now, I witnessed her changing from a dependent woman who had relied on her husband to tell her how to vote to one who was going to call the shots. Can I too change as I age? Can I forsake needing to be in control and allow my body to tell me when it is time to let go? Perhaps when I am eighty, I will choose to forego pneumonia shots, add DNR in red capital letters to my medical chart. I want to believe I can become as fearless as my mother.

Effigyville

by Anton Yakovlev

When the old designer store downtown
went out of business and was razed to the ground,
the moldy crater where it had stood was adorned with posters
illustrating a luminescent housing development
that was about to be erected in its location,
so tall one could almost see England from its top floors.
But when the builders of the new structure went bankrupt,
the posters faded from the seasonal weather changes
and soon were no more than gaping metal boards.
To make some use of them, and to slightly alleviate
the heavy moods of old jewelers strolling the city streets
and ladies with aging dogs peeking out of handbags,
City Hall took charge and put up ornate watercolors
of the imploded designer store, back in its golden years.

Soon families with strollers readjusted their daily walks
to no longer avoid the downtown. The elegant toddlers
found themselves in a reverie, musing about the building
that used to stand there—an activity healthy enough
that no one objected when a similar set of posters
went up down the street, at the site of a former bookstore
that had suddenly run out of customers.

A waterfront natural history museum was next to go.
Its implosion was met with unforeseen geographic
cataclysms, a landslide making the waterfront
disappear along with the building. Nevertheless,

murals were erected, showing in splendid brushstrokes
the glory days of the museum and of the creatures there.

The oldest tavern in town closed down shortly thereafter.
Award-winning musicians were invited to play at its demolition,
timing their melodies with the metronome of the battering ram.
Soon there were resplendent pencil sketches around
demonstrating the tavern's unique Victorian architecture
and the fraternal spirit that had made its customers feel immortal.

The circus was next, then the zoo, then the opera house.
Law firms followed suit. Like a house of cards,
the casino folded. Jails were swiftly dismantled,
sometimes at night, to slow the onset of anarchy.
A house of worship was turned into a swimming pool,
but then there was no more water for people to swim in,
and all that was left was a brand new radiant mural
portraying the house of worship, while a small poster
of the swimming pool curled up near one of its corners.

City Hall was the last to fall: its grand edifice
was the hardest to sketch, so intricately it wove
various dead end corridors, visible even from
the outside of the building—a conscious metaphor
for the way they did business back when there was a city.
Finally, a great artist answered the call,
succeeded at painting the building—and then it was gone.

A cloud of old dust hovering over deserted streets,
the city of murals and posters stood silent in summertime,
offering no spin, no bias, no right way to think
to the amateur photographer that happened to wander

onto the old city streets one day, his battery fully charged.
He tried to take pictures but only took pictures of pictures,
and pictures of pictures had always interested him less
than any other pictures. So he jumped back in his car,
kicking up a cloud of sand with his all-wheel drive,
and turned his attention to the forest of reeds and ferns,
which reached much higher now than the highest penthouse.

The Fatwa on Chess

by Harvey Blume

Saudi Arabia's leading religious authority, Grand Mufti Abdul-Aziz al-Sheikh, last week put a fatwa on chess in advance of a tournament scheduled to be held in the holy city of Mecca.

To be sure, some of his indictments of the game have merit. For example, he calls it "the work of Satan," and who of sound mind, from novice to master, could object, as in who but Lucifer himself could have cooked this game up?

(There is Intelligent Design, and then there is Malign Design. Chess, according to the Mufti, and others, and not without evidence, springs from the latter. It is also said that the Devil invented the violin. And conga drums.)

The Mufti argues, further, that chess "leads to rivalry and enmity." Losing in chess does indeed provoke anxiety and dire imaginings, suicidal and homicidal. This is BFS, Bobby Fischer Syndrome. And Fischer hadn't even lost when he lost his cookies: the very thought of losing — losing, ever, again, even once— was enough to bring out all that was broken and bonkers in him, which was plenty.

Winning was all that could quiet him.

But I'm not yet ready to convert to the Wahhabi version of Islam (or, for some strange reason, any other version) despite the insights of the fatwa-hurling Mufti. I prefer to align myself with Muslim advocates of chess who have tweeted, contra said Mufti, that "chess is an intelligent game and that is why conservative clerics decry it."

And there's no doubt that the Mufti was talking about some other pursuit when he said chess makes "rich people poor and poor people rich." Perhaps he was thinking of backgammon.

Poker.

Oil.

Islam has had a fruitful but conflicted relationship to chess. Muslims both brought the game to Europe — along with the works of Plato and some basics of arithmetic — and shied away from it. They authored the first serious studies of chess, but their tension about it extended to representation of the pieces.

Islam took the second commandment's ban on graven images very seriously. Thus, on their chess sets, the horse, which we call the knight, was not allowed to bear any resemblance to an actual horse; it had to be represented abstractly, by means of an assortment of holes poked into the exterior. Same with the elephant. (Yes, the elephant was once an active piece: Chinese chess, xiangqi, is known, for short, as elephant chess). As for the queen, well, she was no problem for Muslim chess, since there was no queen. There is no queen in Chinese chess either. Make of it what you will, the queen is a European innovation.

It should be said that these abstract Islamic chess pieces are beautiful, in an unexpectedly modern way.

Islam still argues with itself about chess. Chess once stood for Enlightenment reason as opposed to clerical and feudal rule. The Cafe de la Regence was a place where Ben Franklin might be found playing, along with Jean-Jacques Rousseau.

The Saudi/Wahhabist monarchy still contends with a contemporary version of the Cafe de la Regence.

Alas for the Saudi/Wahhabist monarchy.

ZABEL YESSAYAN

We're proud to present, in collaboration with the Zabel Yessayan project, a sampler of the work of this important artist. Born in 1878, Yessayan emerged into the tumultuous, multiethnic world of late 19th century Constantinople at a time when Sultan Abdul Hamid unleashed his fury on both Christian minorities and the progressive elements of Ottoman society.

One of the first women from the Ottoman Empire to study overseas, she traveled to Paris at the age of 17 to study at the Sorbonne. She wrote her first novel, *The Waiting Room*, about an emigre North African Jewish woman. Set in Paris, *The Waiting Room* explores themes that would become central to her work: exile, alienation, and the "Other".

Her influential voice brought her to the attention of the Armenian religious leadership of Constantinople, who asked her to join a delegation to provide relief for the victims of the 1909 massacres of Adana. Upon her return from Adana, she wrote her most powerful appeal for human rights, *In the Ruins*. Her experience in Adana and the uprising in the Balkans shaped her views of war, and in

1912-1913 she wrote *Enough!*, which decried the horror of war on the innocent of both sides. She was the only woman on the list of 250 intellectuals in Constantinople (Istanbul) who were targeted for murder at the early stages of the Armenian Genocide.

Yessayan eluded arrest and went into hiding until she escaped to Bulgaria using a false identity. For the next five years, she travelled and recorded eyewitness testimony from survivors of the Armenian Genocide. She eventually settled in Soviet Armenia in 1933 where she taught literature at the University and continued to write. Her support of fellow Armenian writers caught the attention of Stalin's henchmen. The target of yet another empire, she was exiled and imprisoned in 1937 and died in unknown circumstances, most likely in 1943.

Yessayan crossed ethnic and religious boundaries and fought for human rights while the world collapsed around her. When in 1912, Yessayan saw refugees from the Balkans in Istanbul, she wrote, "They have been ousted from their own lands and turned into refugees....What have we got in common? What makes us similar? When I see the expression of intense fear in their faces my own pain, which had begun to recede, flames up again."

Many thanks to AIWA, the Armenian International Women's Association, which has been translating her work into English, at and has allowed Pangyrus to republish the pieces you see here. Read more about the Zabel Yessayan project at aiwainternational.org.

The House (The Gardens of Silihdar)

by Zabel Yessayan

Top photo: Scutari, Constantinople, Turkey, between ca. 1890 and ca. 1900. Photo from Library of Congress Prints and Photographs Division.

I was born in a typical, two-story wooden house that had been painted red. The windows looking out onto the street had curtains that were almost always closed, because, just in front of our house was a Greek grocery that doubled as a tavern.

The members of my family would spend the day in the rooms towards the back of the house, where the windows opened out onto a series of groves.

Beyond those groves lay the Turkish neighborhoods. In those neighborhoods were magnificent mosques whose slim, white minarets joined black cypress trees on the skyline. From a distance, the glistening blue Bosphorus looked like a ribbon and the silhouette of Stamboul—shrouded in a pink mist in the morning, a golden mist during the day and a blue mist in the evening—looked like a colorful, ever-changing, ethereal wonderland.

Scutari Rooftops, Constantinople, Turkey. Photo from the Princeton Library.

As a child, I was dazzled by the rays of light that seemed to catch fire as they reflected off the golden domes of the mosques. That vibrant, yet subtle panorama was the first to make a profound visual impression on me. Even before I could articulate my thoughts, these impressions produced powerful emotions in me — inspiring both laughter and tears — and later in life, when I saw the same sights again, I felt like I had already experienced them.

I remember spring mornings when those groves — the Gardens of Silihdar — were transformed into a paradise filled with fiery roses in bloom. Those roses overran the house; they adorned bare rooms, brought fragrance and color to white walls, and became toys for children. Their petals rained down on everything and everyone.

I remember how the wisteria tumbled down the trellis and, like a luxurious cape, masked the gloom of houses that had fallen into disrepair. Sunlight filtered through the leafy trees and created fleeting patterns on the ground. The cool breeze passed over people and plants like a caress and made young branches sway playfully.

I remember the warm, feverish nights, the sound of croaking frogs rising from the pond, the buzzing of the fireflies, and the endless creaking of the artesian wells that seeped into my dreams, even during those sick, restless nights I often endured as a child. Sometimes I would hear a gardener from the steppes of Rumelia sing a distant, nostalgic song with a shepherd's fife in hand.

I remember my suffering before the beauty of nature and my powerless yearning to possess what were only scents, colors, lights and dreams.

I loved to look closely at the sky as the white clouds outlined in gold slowly changed shape. I would occasionally see part of a larger cloud separate from the rest and float quickly through the blue sky. All of this came to life before my eyes and, with the limited understanding of a child, I gave meaning to those movements and transformations as I fixed my eyes on the fiery western horizon and the reddish bands sketched above it.

I remember the cool May rain that would fall in a hurried patter on the thirsty plants and red tile roofs. The rainwater used to gush from the gutters onto the wet, crumbling ground and create countless streams and tributaries in it. From the open windows, a fresh breath of crisp air would rush inside. The smell of newly plowed gardens and groves, fertile land and wet plants would spread through the air. And in the morning, the dew-covered flowers, satiated by the rain, smiled in that garden.

I remember walking along the small path in our garden and stepping on the spots of light that trembled in the shadows of the swaying branches. I remember the vague unease that suddenly took hold of me as I listened intently to the rustling of the trees and the whisper of the streams.

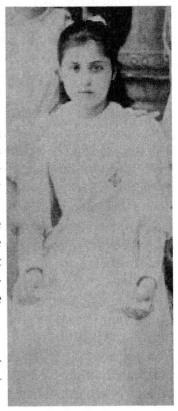

In that garden, royal apricot trees offered me their golden fruit. Blooming rosebushes anointed my childhood with their sweet fragrance and, with the light touch of my fingertips, beautiful red and white rose petals fell to my feet.

Over the course of my life, I have seen many places and have enjoyed the beauty of nature in many forms, but my memories of the Gardens of Silihdar have remained indelible. I have

* * *

Zabel Yessayan, possibly at graduation. Photo courtesy of the Museum of Literature and Art, Yerevan, Armenia.

carried those gardens with me everywhere, and in them I have found refuge every time dark, menacing clouds have accumulated on my horizon.

Although outside, the garden and neighboring groves were filled with smiles and laughter, inside it was cold and gloomy.

My grandmother's strict cleaning habits drove out any object that could have brought a small amount of pleasant disorder or whimsy into our lives. The walls of every room were plastered and painted white. All the rooms had wood floors, except for two, which were covered in straw mats. These floors were washed and scrubbed so often that our noses grew accustomed to the smell of wet wood.

At the back of each room, a divan—always covered in a white blanket—stretched from one side of the room to the other. The windows were dressed in white curtains ironed into crisp pleats. A round table covered in a white crocheted tablecloth held a water pitcher and a glass overturned on a crystal plate. We would eat our meals on the patio, which was paved with white marble. At night, we slept in white nightgowns on mattresses with rose and lavender scented sheets that were spread across the floor. Everything in our house was white as far as the eye could see.

There were no pictures on the walls, or any vases in any of the rooms. In Doudou's eyes, my aunts were defiling the house any time they brought flowers from the garden and put them in jars. Only when the roses were in bloom did flowers fill the house in large numbers. Doudou could only tolerate the scent of roses, which she said smelled fresh. To her, other scents—both natural and artificial—were simply unacceptable for virtuous people.

Once winter arrived and the doors to the garden were closed, despair gripped my young soul.

Curled up on a white divan and nestled close to one of my aunts, I used to yearn for those rosebushes and the sunny, winding paths of our garden. I used to close my eyes and tell myself stories about roses who could talk and trees who frolicked down the street, almost forming a circle dance with their outstretched branches.

I was rarely allowed to enter the two places of refuge in the house. The first was Aunt Yeranig's room where she worked alone on her *yazmas*. Aunt Yeranig was fiercely protective of her privacy. For me, her room was a mysterious sanctuary, and the joy of entering it was almost impossible to attain. The second was the largest room in the house where my aunts worked on their yazmas at their workbenches, sometimes together, sometimes alone.

For me, that room was full of wonder. The floor was covered in straw mats that creaked slightly under my aunts' slippers; the divan was covered in colorful fabric, and the yellow curtains in the room were decorated with thick red stripes.

Their workbenches were the objects of my greatest curiosity. They were low tables in front of which my aunts Youghaper and Makrig—dressed in yellow, pink or blue *entaris* with big, colorful flowers—would sit cross-legged on cushions as they worked on their yazmas.

Along one side of the workbenches were clay bowls with red, yellow and purple paint. Only Aunt Yeranig used green and blue.

The leaves and flowers sketched on the yazmas would be given color and texture as soon as my aunts dipped their brushes in a color and started working. Chatting as they worked, my aunts would hang their painted yazmas in rows. They exposed my curious mind to the outside world. I did not understand most of what they discussed, but my newly stirred imagination nonetheless took flight and created a new world for myself with the fragments of their conversations.

I felt a special kind of love for my Aunt Youghaper, or Gogo as I called her. She was the oldest of her sisters and acted like a mother not only to me, but to my own mother. She was the one who looked after me, bathed me, dressed me and put me to bed at night. Gogo, with her dainty appearance, light chestnut-colored hair and dark eyes set deep in their sockets, took meticulous care of herself. Her hair was cut into bangs that fell to her eyebrows, and she was the only woman in the house who powdered her face with rice powder, despite the criticism she received for it. She also liked colorful fabrics. I remember that she had wanted to make a red velvet dress for many years, but never managed to do it, because her mother's rigid opinions ruled over the house. Gogo would sometimes fall into a deep depression and, as if she were holding a grudge against the other members of the family, would work sadly and sullenly with her left hand pressed to her temple, since on those days her nervous facial tic would intensify. I would watch as tears silently rolled down her sunken cheeks. That portrait of sadness weighed heavily on my heart and tormented me. I did not know what to do to bring a smile to Gogo's hopeless face, but from time to time I managed to do it. If she was in a good mood, Gogo was sweet and affectionate. I have never heard as many tender words as I have from her. Throughout our entire routine—dressing, undressing, etcetera—she never stopped enveloping me in loving whispers. She made all of my wishes come true with a kind of patience that knew no bounds. She would gently comb my hair, and to keep me busy, tell stories or sing in a soft, sad voice.

Aunt Makrig, on the other hand, had an impetuous personality. Her moods could change in an instant. Having a love for life and a cheerful disposition, but deprived of the same opportunities her brothers had to indulge themselves outside the home, she would sometimes erupt in a sudden rage and rebel—even against her mother—over something quite trivial.

She married late in life, only after her mother's death. Her husband was a pathetic man for whom she harbored legitimate contempt until his death. But it was through that marriage that Aunt Makrig found independence and began a life that brought her endless happiness. Every evening, a tray of *oghi* would be prepared; guests, musicians and neighbors—both Armenian and Turkish—would gather and spend a delightful evening singing and playing music together.

If it so happened that a disagreeable neighbor complained about the festivities, and those grumblings reached Aunt Makrig, she would immediately put the neighbor in his or her place.

On short winter days when my aunts worked by the light of a lantern, my mother would sometimes carry me or take me by the hand into their workroom. In that room, they had installed a stove in order to dry the yazmas more quickly. The wood crackled in the fire and the lanterns flickered. The smell of paint coupled with the images I had sketched in my mind from my aunts' conversations made me dizzy. My father would sometimes come home late. He would often work until midnight in his workshop, and occasionally, when he did, my aunts would forget to put me to bed. One by one, my uncles would return home from work—or more often from the tavern—and start talking about their jobs, their bosses and the men and women with whom they worked.

Aunt Makrig and my uncles—Aunt Youghaper was too good-natured and understanding—used to mercilessly ridicule their boss, Chevigents Partig. Partig's brother Tateos was thought to be a complete fool and was nicknamed Aré in the neighborhood. My uncles would describe Aré's exploits in the market and in the streets with big, hearty laughs. Occasionally, they would tell old stories about their father and uncles. I would listen to these stories as if they were the most marvelous tales ever told. My joy would reach its peak when Uncle Dikran returned home from the tavern. Gangan, as I called him, had a dazzling personality. While his brothers Bedros and Boghos, always looking for a fight, would cause mayhem whenever they had too much to drink, Gangan was a happy drunk.

When he came home, Gangan would take me in his arms, lift me all the way to the ceiling and joke around with everyone in the room. And sometimes, stretched out on a straw mat, he would recite a *destan* or sing one of his own *ashough* songs. He used to write poetry in Turkish with Armenian letters; I managed to save some of his poems, and I have kept them to this day.

Uncle Dikran was well educated and knew modern Armenian, classical Armenian and Turkish very well. After graduating from the Sourp Khatch School in Scutari, he worked as a secretary for a Turkish merchant from Trabzon. One day, he left his job unexpectedly to wander through Anatolia, finally returning to Constantinople in a dreadful state. He later entered the yazma business and became a textile worker like his brothers Boghos and Bedros. In the heat of the summer and the bitter cold of the winter, they would all walk down to the shore to wash the yazmas and climb back up the hill with the wet yazmas on their shoulders. They would prepare them to be painted, distribute them among the neighbors and go to the tavern every night to console themselves after a hard day's work.

Gangan was a handsome man with dark eyes, thick black hair and a bushy mustache. When he was half-drunk, he would whisper stories in my ear about *khabadayis* and their adventures. He would also tell me tales of other brave men who, rebelling against injustice, would disappear into the mountains and become *eshguias*. Uncle Dikran talked about these eshguias with so much admiration that, for a very long time, I thought that the noblest men in the world were bandits who took refuge in the mountains. Whenever Doudou listened to his stories, she would furrow her brow and stare off into the distance. If Gangan noticed Doudou's stern expression, he would say half-seriously, half-jokingly:

—What's wrong, Doudou? Are you unhappy?

Expressing her disdain, my grandmother's pale lips did not deign to respond.

More often, Gangan would lament the powerlessness of his generation.

—Are we really Shirine's grandchildren? Who would have thought that those tigers of men would bear housecats like us? Are we not men, too? Aré's brother takes us by the nose and drags us wherever he likes. Cursed is this worthless life.

One winter evening past midnight, Gangan brought home a tobacco smuggler who was wanted by the government. Smugglers were usually Circassian, but a few Armenians had started to join forces with them. Uncle Dikran established ties with these smugglers; his adventurous spirit seemed to invigorate them. The smugglers were armed and were constantly fighting against the government, especially against the French government, which had a monopoly on the tobacco industry at the time. The farmers who grew tobacco in the villages around Constantinople tried to help them in any way they could. The government officials and gendarmes called in to subdue the smugglers were chosen from similarly brave men who were under strict orders to show no mercy. The heroic battles that ensued would take place just outside of Scutari and would always end in bloodshed.

The members of my family were stunned by Gangan's audacity. I think I remember the fugitive's face: sharp like the blade of a sword with small, sparkling eyes and a swarthy complexion. I was barely four years old at the time.

When the fugitive left three days later, my father talked to Doudou about Uncle Dikran's behavior. He had decided to become an eshguia and had plans to disappear into the mountains. They both thought he needed to be stopped and hastily married him to the daughter of a fisherman named Nigot with the hope that he would settle down and put an end to his perpetual wandering.

Gangan never left Scutari again and, the more time passed, the more heavily he drank. Sometimes, he would pound on our door late at night in a drunken stupor and wake up the entire household with his ramblings about the unrealized ambitions of his youth. He would later sigh deeply and cry:

—Shame on us for calling ourselves Shirine's grandchildren. Look at him and look at us! We are the unworthy products of our time.

Translated by Jennifer Manoukian.

In the Ruins

by Zabel Yessayan

Top photo: Destruction of the Armenian quarter in Adana. From Armenian Genocide Museum-Institute, Yerevan, Armenia.

Under a superb, dazzling sun, the devastated city stretches outward like a cemetery without end. Ruins everywhere... Nothing has been spared; all the churches, schools, and dwellings have been reduced to formless piles of charred stone, among which, here and there, the skeletons of buildings jut up. From east to west, from north to south, all the way to the distant limits of the Turkish quarters, an implacable, ferocious hatred has burned and destroyed everything. Over this deathly wasteland and these immense piles of ash, two minarets, unscathed, rise arrogantly toward the sky.

Draped in rags stained with blood and tears, a crowd of widows, orphans, and old people presents itself to us. This is all that is left of Adana's Armenian population. The crowd has the sullen calm of a sea that has fallen still after a big storm; its pain and inconsolable sorrow are hidden in its depths and rise only fitfully to the surface. The hope of living, of being reborn, has been snuffed out in these people. And if hunger and thirst had not shaken them out of their stupor, life would already have been extinguished in them for good.

Survivors standing amid destroyed homes. Armenian Genocide Museum-Institute, Yerevan, Armenia

They keep silent for a long time, as if following the thread of their memories, involuntarily carried away by their ghastly course and breathing heartfelt sighs that seem to rip through their breasts: "Aman…" Sometimes they break out in sobs. In an instant, their cheeks are flooded by such an abundance of gushing tears that their words of protest and complaint are drowned out. Then their faces, faces wizened and bronzed by work in the sun, are furrowed by terrible wrinkles and contorted in frightful grimaces, and the whole crowd writhes in despair, prey to a fit of inconsolable grief. It is impossible to imagine what portion of that crowd's sorrow each particular individual represents.

Indeed, it is impossible to grasp or feel the atrocious reality all at once. It exceeds the limits of the human imagination. Even those who experienced that reality cannot give an account of it as a whole. They all stammer, sigh, weep, and recount only disconnected events. Despair and terror had reached such heights that mothers failed to recognize their children, and crippled or blind old people were forgotten in houses that had been set ablaze. Listening to a savage, bloodthirsty mob's diabolical, raucous laughter, people lost their minds before dying. Mangled limbs and children's bodies still throbbing with life and pain were trampled underfoot. Trapped between rifle fire on the one hand and flames on the other, women, children, and the wounded who had taken refuge in churches and schools wrapped their arms around each other as, crazy with fear, they were burned black.

Yet neither those stories, nor the scattered Armenians milling about in those ashes, nor the orphans with their grief-stricken, bewildered eyes and the expressions of children still dazed with terror on their faces, nor the bodies of the bereaved widows writhing over their irreparable loss, nor even the amputees' painful, still open wounds capture the dark enormity of what actually happened in those hellish days. It is in people's anxious, terror-stricken eyes that sometimes, for a moment, I think I can catch a glimpse of it. Oh, those eyes! Some appear to have been struck blind and to have renounced the joys of the sun forever; they seem as empty as bottomless chasms. Some look at you without seeing, because one image has been indelibly impressed on their field of vision. Some have preserved the rhythm of the ghastly flames in their gaze. And some, with pupils in constant motion, pupils tormented by haunting scenes of fire and bloodshed, seem to long for blindness and peace.

It was in that crowd that I saw the grieving figure of Missak's mother. Stalked by the nightmare of her hanged son, beating her breast, tearing at her rags, she sang the praises of her martyred child and, as if thirsting for tears, kept crying, "My eyes are springs run dry...my children! I have been consumed by the fire in my heart...my children...aman!"

I saw mothers there who had strangled their babies so that their infant cries would not betray them in their hiding places. I saw women there who, paralyzed, their tongues lolling on their chins, were unable to cry out their heart's grief. I saw madwomen who, rather than forgetting, endlessly relived the terrible moment: they were haunted by memories of their loved ones falling one after the other, and did not know which one to mourn... "They lined them up over there, one next to the other, and they fired and they fired and they fired, and all of them tottered for a moment, like this, and then they toppled to the ground. It was my father and my husband and my sons, and now I'm all alone, like an owl amid the ruins. Akh..."

Sometimes they seem indifferent, as if the intensity of their grief had turned them to stone. With calm faces on which not a muscle stirs, they relate the dreadful facts. Every word they utter is spilled blood.

Then, suddenly, they pause; their eyes gleam with a crazy

light — what image has flashed before their mind's eye? — and they cry out, beside themselves, clinging to our emotion, imploring help from our tears and kindred feelings…

Destruction of the Armenian quarter in Adana. Photo from Armenian Genocide Museum-Institute, Yerevan, Armenia.

In the ruined city, in their ruined hearts, everything has been destroyed. In my imagination, I can still see the gesture of a crazed village woman: summing up everything that had happened in their village with a sweeping movement of her hand, she repeated, mechanically, "If you want to believe it, believe it; if you don't want to, don't. Everything is over, everything is finished."

In this nameless catastrophe, it is not the charred houses or devastated gardens that seem past saving and past reclaiming; nor is it the large numbers of the dead and dying. Rather, it is that crippling inner feeling drifting through everyone's eyes — a feeling of misery, of despondency. It is the feeling of a people that has been trodden underfoot, that has been crushed under the soles of brutes. Heads that, thirsting for light and freedom, had for a moment been lifted in human dignity have been smashed with ruthless cruelty. Tortured by this thought, I look out at the demolished city, whose heaps of charred rubble take on a different and terrible meaning. And yet, amid this sinister desolation and despair, a smile of hope blooms.

In the ruins, a group of women has taken refuge in the shade of the partly demolished walls. Suspended between one wall and another, a cradle is gently rocking. Who knows? What the violence of our grief presents as impossible is perhaps possible after all for the people's untiring, unconscious genius for rebirth. For that wretched child's humble cradle, indifferent to the immense general calamity and quick with an invincible instinct for life, is rocking above this vast cemetery, perfectly indifferent to both the martyred people's abject misery and the criminals' monstrous savagery.

Translated by G. M. Goshgarian.

The Man
Memories from My Student Years

by Zabel Yessayan

– For Adrushan[1]

"In terror, there is a kind of sublime, delightful pleasure," a friend once told me, showing me Adrushan's beautiful article in *Masis*.[2] It is as if all of our senses suddenly awaken. There is something I don't understand in that limitless, intoxicating feeling of panic, something that often only lasts for a moment, but whose memory continues to vibrate in our souls.

We argued a bit. Yes, the most overwhelming, powerful, intoxicating feeling was terror; I could accept that. But I could not accept the idea that terror could bring about pleasure. And in order to explain what I was saying, I told my friend about something that had happened to me, about a memory from my student years that often comes to mind.

It was the beginning of my second year in Paris. At that time, I lived on Boulevard Arago in a small room on the sixth floor overlooking a courtyard. The courtyard and the buildings surrounding it created a small square-shaped shaft as deep as a well. From six stories high, I couldn't see the ground. That shaft was dotted with small windows from which the nauseating smell of poorly pre-pared food would waft out twice a day and constantly hang in the air. Above me, all I could see was a square-shaped sky, and that too was often covered by black, noxious smoke from the nearby factories or by a cheerless, muggy haze. When, once in a while, I would see the blue of the sky, my soul would fill with childish joy; in those moments, it seemed that all people needed to feel pure, unadulterated happiness was a bright, blue sky.

Sometimes from the depths of the courtyard, through the stench of cooked meat and suspicious greasy particles that coated the four sides of the shaft, the voice of a singing vagabond would rise and take hold of the area. Whenever I heard him, I would put my work aside, go to the window, and dream. Oh, how I would dream. If the strangled, sobbing sound of a barrel organ would reach me, I don't know why, but a strange sadness would pass through my soul, and I would feel a sentimental urge to cry in my dark, gloomy room.

I felt hopeless and bitter, and I was entirely alone to bear it all and ruminate on my worries. In that sad, freezing room, I would look out the window at night and feel as though I was on the edge of a dark, gaping pit. In the house, workers and their families lived on the first five floors; the sixth floor, made up of small rooms, was entirely occupied by foreign students—sad, blonde girls who would wearily trudge up six flights of stairs. Yet on their pale, mel-ancholy faces, the light of vigor and determination shone steadily and continually in their eyes.

We would smile at one another and even say hello sometimes, but I didn't have any kind of relationship with any one of them. At night, when they would all gather in one room, I would listen to the wistful, heartbroken cadences of their foreign songs, or to the weak, tender vibrations of the mandolin. And only during those hours did all of my strength, all of my unshakable ambition, all of my fanatical determination to persevere melt like a snowflake, and I would feel the chill of despair in my soul. Oh, that soft staccato of the mandolin. It is as if its debilitating vibrations will always stay with me, and remind me of my weaknesses and disappointments in my dreary room on Boulevard Arago.

I've said that at the time I was in a hopeless, bitter state, so it's easy to understand when I say that not one of my compatriots ever came to visit me. I would spend days, sometimes weeks, without uttering a single word in my language. (It was in that state that I lost my habit of thinking in Armenian). I had a few foreign acquaintances, but almost all of them were also students, and extremely busy with their exams. As a result, I lived a more isolated existence than ever before, and outside the time I spent working, I immersed myself in the writing of Edgar Allen Poe. For quite a while, I read a lot of Poe, and Baudelaire.[3]

Their books were the ones on my night table, and before going to sleep, I would slowly recite a sonnet from *Les Fleurs du Mal*. It was as if these sonnets were an intoxicating, unsettling drink I would consume drop by drop. I'm saying all of this to more clearly express the emotional state I found myself in on the morning Miss Zavatska—one of my foreign friends—came to my room, pale and terrified.

"Oh, you have no idea. You can't possibly understand the strange thing that just happened to me. I can't stay in this house. I just can't anymore. One of these nights, my terror and fear will kill me."

Almost sobbing, she muttered some incoherent words, among which I could make out only "Terrifying! It's something really horrifying."

Miss Zavatska was a lovely young girl. She was a literature student like me whom I met in Deschanel's class. Very blond and very dainty, Zavatska suffered from a malady of the chest. Her years were numbered and she knew it. What I didn't understand—really couldn't understand —was why she had decided to spend her fleeting youth in one of Paris's poor, student neighborhoods. In other words, why was she enduring a life full of hardship and deprivation, when the depth of that life, containing a bitter, special kind of pleasure, would be entirely inaccessible to her shy, wistful, delicate soul?

So Zavatska told me what happened:

"The other day after midnight, there was a knock at my door. I woke up suddenly and shouted, 'Who is it?' There was no answer. Naturally, I said to myself that I must have heard the noise in a dream and confused it with reality. Who could it really have been at that hour? I stayed awake for a short time and listened to make sure no one was there. I didn't hear anything, so I fell back asleep. Some time had passed when I awoke suddenly. There was someone at the door again! This time I listened, my heart pounding. The bell of the Broca Hospital across the street rang three times. It was three o'clock in the morning! My forehead was drenched in cold sweat. A feeling of alarm and danger seized me once more, but again I thought, 'There's nobody there. It just seems like it.' And I was just about to convince myself of that, when this time I heard three powerful thuds on my door. In that moment, everything around me was so silent that the city almost seemed empty. My heart was beating so hard that, for a minute, I thought the thuds I had heard earlier had been my own heartbeats. But no, there was no way to confuse the two. The three thuds on my door were much louder. And at the same time, I could hear a man breathing—a rasping, muffled, ominous kind of breathing. What could I do? My room was pitch black, but opening my eyes wide, I could slowly make out the outline of the furniture. And during all that time, I sensed that there was someone outside my door. I stayed like that—tense and terrified—for a while. The breathing soon faded away, and

I heard muted footsteps, as if someone was walking carefully in socks. I couldn't sleep for the rest of the night, and when morning came..."

"Wait a minute," I said, interrupting her. "This is a kind of fear a child would describe, Zavatska. Surely it was a flirtatious neighbor who had seen you, and thinking you were one of the girls from the factory, wanted to try ..."

"I thought the exact same thing once it was light outside, and I heard that everyone in the house was awake. Thinking about the night before, I saw that there was nothing in the room to make it seem as if anything had happened. It's even funny to tell people about something so vague. But fear had already been sown in my heart, and the following night it was hard for me to get to sleep.

"I woke up as the Broca Hospital bell was ringing midnight, and I'm sure it was for no reason at all. But all my senses were in such a state of excitement that it was as if I was hearing a cacophony of noises and seeing bright, ever-changing shapes. Suddenly the same soft, dull sound of footsteps—I don't know where they came from—approached my room. Yes, it was the exact same sound. There was no doubt about it. Soon I heard the same breathing—muffled and ominous. It was as if I was hanging off a cliff; I felt the same strange feeling that would often overwhelm me in my dreams. Instinctively, as a way to protect myself, I had lost the ability to sense the passing of time, but a couple of thuds jolted me back to reality.

" 'Who is it,' I shouted without thinking.

" 'Miss,' a voice outside the door stammered. 'Can you lend me some matches? Please, I beg you. I'm completely in the dark.'

" 'I don't have any,' I said abruptly in a dry tone.

" 'Miss, I'm your neighbor. If you do have some, could you please lend me one or two, because I forgot to get them and...'

"And then I heard the sound of my lock, which he was turning in vain. I had drawn the bolt, but I was sure that ruffian, that criminal (who knows what he was) could somehow get the door open. Lying in bed, I was as cold as a corpse, and my limbs had cramped and stiffened. I wanted to get up, get dressed, open my window, and call for help, but I couldn't do anything. All these ideas passed through my mind, ran through my mind, without having a single effect on me.

"And I stayed like that for I don't know how long. There were a few more attempts to open the door until finally the raspy breathing faded away, and the footsteps disappeared into the nearby courtyard.

"In the morning, I went downstairs to complain to the doorman.

" 'All of your neighbors are upstanding people. Something like that couldn't have happened,' he told me. Yet I explained what had happened in greater detail. It was the absolute truth. But the man shook his head stubbornly.

" 'It couldn't have happened, Miss. No one could have done that to you.'

" 'But...'

"His wife came in, so I had to tell the story again. This time, they started to laugh as if what I was saying was funny.

" 'What a strange girl! It's all in your head. Who in this house would want to come ask you for matches at three o'clock in the morning?'

"And one by one, they listed my neighbors—decent people in their mind. I didn't know any one of them.

" 'Fine,' I said to myself once I left the house and found myself out in the fresh air. 'I seem to be ill.' I was subjected to surprising nervous weaknesses, but my God, everything was so clear. I wanted to see my doctor and be treated for it, but I couldn't find him. Last night, I reluctantly returned to my room, but luckily Miss S came and stayed with me until midnight. I didn't tell her anything, but after she left, I drew the bolt and made sure it was secure. Then I drank a lot of rum to try to fall into a deep sleep. I fell asleep as soon as I lay down.

"Again? There was no question this time that there was a man outside my door, because I could see a very distinct strip of light in the narrow gap between the door and the doorframe. I knew it. Almost panting, the man worked to open the door. There was no way not to believe it. I heard the soft, careful sound of his tools, especially the gentle, rhythmic scraping of his file. And then," Zavatska turned entirely white, "the door opened. It was still dark, but humid air from outside rushed into the room like a torrent, and the breathing drew closer —the raspy panting of a wild animal, carefully and softly tip-toeing his way towards my bed.

"In the morning, I found myself sprawled out on the floor. I had fainted and had been there for hours. My entire body hurt and my limbs were as stiff as a corpse's. Once I remembered what had happened, I jumped up, terrified. I don't even know how I got myself dressed, but it was certainly hastily because my clothes and sheets were thrown everywhere.

"My door was closed as usual and the bolt was in place. I don't know how it could be. I came straight here. You have to understand. I can't spend the night there. It would be impossible. Impossible!"

Zavatska, terribly distraught, started to cry like a little child.

I thought for a moment. I could easily believe what the poor girl was saying. She had a look of genuine terror on her face, but there was something about her story that also inspired some doubt in my mind.

"Was everything in the right place when you woke up in the morning? Was anything out of order? Your drawers or anything like that?"

"Not a thing. Everything was in exactly the same place, except for me. I had fallen onto the floor with my sheets."

"And you said that the door was bolted from the inside."

"It definitely was. I checked before I opened the door to come see you, and I was surprised."

"You know, Zavatska," I said holding her cold hands, "it seems as if your mind might have been playing tricks on you these past few nights."

"Oh, no, no! Don't talk to me like the doorman did. You have to understand what I'm saying."

"Fine, do you want me to come over tonight and stay with you?"

After some hesitation, Zavatska accepted my offer.

Naturally, it wasn't my courage I was relying on to get through the night. I was convinced that Zavatska was having a nervous breakdown. Fear had never penetrated my soul until that point; I had never been subjected to a truly gripping, deadly kind of terror.

And yet all day I thought about what had happened to Zavatska. If it was true, the idea was like a poisonous bite that shook me to my core many times over.

In the evening, we had dinner together, and after going for a walk, we came back to her room. By the time the water for tea had started to boil on the alcohol burner, we seemed to have forgotten everything, and started telling each other about memories from back home—sweet, fragrant memories. Mine were bright and shone golden in the sun, and hers were calm and tender like a melody. We were so far from home and so foreign to each other, yet we felt so close in that moment, almost like sisters. There was so much shared affection in our words, and in our gestures.

Poor Zavatska, do you remember the night the doctor's prediction came true? When nothing, nothing more, remained of your dainty, blonde head, or your clear, bright eyes?

When it came time to go to bed, we had completely forgotten about the nightmare that Zavatska called *The Man* in a special tone of voice, and we even started making jokes about it.

"Now let's go to bed and wait for *The Man*."

"I'm sure *The Man* saw you and now won't come tonight. You'll see!"

"Thanks for the compliment, Zavatska. Am I so terrifying that I can send *The Man* running?"

"Oh dear, I didn't mean it like that."

Later, to get me to go to sleep, Zavatska made me drink half a bottle of rum almost by force. She drank the rest.

"I'm so drunk," I told her. "It wouldn't surprise me if *Men* started appearing before my eyes. I'm sure you're feeling the same way."

This time I was right. The room was filled with cigar smoke, and after I drank the half-bottle of rum in one gulp, I felt like everything was spinning in a bright circle dance around me.

I was lying down on a big armchair across from Zavatska's bed. We kept talking after turning out the lights, and because I was trying to convince Zavatska to ease up on the strong drinks, she tried to convince me of the opposite, saying:

"Rum, you see, is harmless and so useful for poor students. In fact, if rum hadn't existed, I wouldn't have been able to last this long. It's true that…"

A deep, heavy sleep pulled my eyelids shut.

I awoke suddenly, and sat up in my bed.

"What is it?" I would have said had my tongue not felt so thick in my mouth. And instead I fell silently back onto my pillow. Zavatska was sleeping soundly. Why did I wake up? What was wrong, I thought to myself. The room was pitch black. Having opened my eyes like a blind person, I had scanned the entire room in vain before noticing a long, bright strip of light near the door.

First it was flickering, but it became steady, and I could hear the scraping of the file—soft, but determined—on the iron lock.

Suddenly the idea that what Zavatska had told me was true filled me with such a strange, vague sense of unease that I felt as if I was being set aflame one minute, and the next I felt a cold sweat creeping up my spine and making me shudder.

Back in reality, the city was silent. It almost seemed deserted. Only the sound of wagons rumbling sinisterly in the distance could be heard from time to time. And at our door *The Man*—this time real and ominous—was grinding his file on the iron lock. Zavatska—feeling safer with me in the room—was still sleeping, and I didn't dare try to wake her up, or to have her share in the terror that was gradually growing in me and making me insane.

Slowly the door started to creak. Yes, that couldn't be denied. And *The Man's* low, raspy breathing was now synchronized with the sound of the grinding metal.

Then the file stopped. I stared at the door, my eyes wide open. The strip of light flickered, and then vanished. At that moment, I can't even express the utter terror I felt. It was a kind of terror that seemed to freeze the blood in my veins. And at that moment, the door opened. In the darkness of the room, an even darker silhouette appeared and slowly came towards me. A gust of freezing, humid air rushed in through the half-open door and froze the sweat on my forehead. As still as a corpse, I stared at the black silhouette, which was silently inching closer. I wouldn't have thought this shapeless blob was human, if not for the wheezing, shallow sound of his breath, whose warmth I could practically feel on my frozen face.

It was as if those were my final moments alive; I felt that the terror I was experiencing in that instant was about to kill me. If it had not been for the beating of my heart, which was pounding so hard in my terrified body, I would have thought that everything had ended for me.

The Man came even closer, and as the minutes passed, I opened my eyes wider in fear until I realized that, in my attempt to see everything, my eyes were shimmering in the light, and that *The Man* could see them. I shut my eyes, and beneath my tepid eyelids, I sensed that my pupils also were frozen. I don't remember how many seconds, or hours, all of it lasted, but when I opened my eyes again, a sad, pale sunrise had given everything a hazy, gray hue. And *The Man* wasn't in the room. Zavatska was still sleeping. A little while later, I heard reassuring footsteps on the stairs. I wanted to get up, but I couldn't. And I put my exhausted head back on my pillow.

When Zavatska woke up, she wanted to joke around again.

"Didn't I say that tonight *The Man*…"

But turning to me, she suddenly got up, and anxiously asked:

"What is it? What's wrong with you? Why are you so pale? Tell me what happened!"

I caught a glimpse of myself in a shard of a mirror, and I was as white as a ghost. My teeth were chattering, and under my eyes were big, black circles.

"Zavatska, you shouldn't stay in this house. What you said is true."

After that, Zavatska had to stay in the hospital for a few months for her nervous breakdowns and frequent delusions. *The Man* had appeared repeatedly during these breakdowns. I also suffered for a long time, and the truth is that even now I don't know if *The Man* was real or if I had simply found myself inside of one of Zavatska's nightmares.

[1] Adrushan is the pen name of Simeon Yeremian (1871-1936), a writer and critic of nineteenth and twentieth-century Armenian literature best known for his 10-volume study *National Figures: Armenian Writers* (in Armenian).

[2] *Masis* was an Armenian newspaper and literary journal based in Constantinople.

[3] Charles Baudelaire (1821-1867), a French poet best known for his *Les Fleurs du Mal* (Flowers of Evil), was also the first to translate the work of Edgar Allan Poe into French. It was through Baudelaire's French translations that Yessayan became acquainted with Poe's work.

Boxwood Hedge

by Melissa Ginsburg

Citizens, drive!

from radioactive waters
in the Southern provinces, arthritic
still and disappointed.

O neighbors and colleagues
Come out of your FourRunners, etc.
Empty your cars of your selves
smelling of sulfur.

This boxwood hedge
thickens like a moat
around an army stormed town.
They call that the ghetto

and stock it with Jews. Come home.
Watch the polite moat

decline its feeding spring. It's mud
under bridges now
and that's what keeps it safe.
See the hedge resembling me?

It grows that way. They all
will, now. That's my gift. Lie under it,
Jews in your country estates

big as hotels, in your spas

at *Baden bei Wien* where you take
the waters
and your hysterical daughters.
I am the post office now,

and you will never send a greater letter.
Lie down now. I'm the cure.

Heartache

by Katie Green

She had used the word like a child in a fairy tale: rattlesnake, bone break, morning wake, milkshake. There are words we use, words we skid along the surface of, words we sway to the rhythm of, that we droop to, that we dance to, but still they are outside of us. We might go a lifetime and know nothing of these words, till we hit them at such impact that we shatter them and pass through, bleeding on the cut glass of their meaning.

And so it was. The heartache hummed in her, turned her lungs to liquid, deepened in her down to the navel up to the throat. It had width, the heartache, it had height and volume. There were days where it might be, say, only three centimeters across and five centimeters high, and other days where it took the entire width of her chest and spread around the sides of her body to her back and clasped hands at her spine, such an embrace of heartache that the therapist, made anxious by her description of the pain, sent her for an EKG to check for cardiac function. And the EKG came back fine, which when she thought about it, was remarkable. For the heart to be fine. And ache so.

Dear Rhiannon

by Jennifer Perrine

Dear Rhiannon,

Bless you for believing when I said I'd backup danced
for Paula Abdul. Bless your sister, who barely arched
an eyebrow when you, all awe, shared the story I'd spun.

New kid in town, I invented a past to shimmy
my way into your skinny, strawberry-blonde, hip-hop
heart, to smother that other history: the hustle

of my mother, the twelve steps of rehab, the shuffle
from one home to the next. This fiction, the only sway
I held, I ran it into the ground, choreographed

our dates so you'd never see the shed where I slept, shook
off your requests. In your room, I'd crack open the rock
of my lie, show you its glittering insides. You'd grind

against that jagged part of me, honing your own slide
into a new life, where you'd ditch your sister's place, swirl
around a pole, your hair dragging the ground when you'd flip

upside down. Or that's how we'd imagined it. I skipped
out after the night you dialed the music up loud, turned
a pirouette, remnant of childhood lessons, and dipped

into an arabesque, leapt, reached for me as you whirled.
Bless you for never mentioning how I stumbled, dropped
my clumsy feet beside your fleet kicks. Bless the rhythm,

how you got lost in it, radiant, while I got down
on my knees, numb and bruised, and prayed for a truer tune
to sing to you, for a tongue brave enough for the blues.

PREPPERS

BY AARON WHITAKER

/'prepər/ *noun.* A PERSON WHO BELIEVES A CATASTROPHIC DISASTER OR EMERGENCY IS LIKELY TO OCCUR IN THE FUTURE & MAKES ACTIVE PREPARATIONS FOR IT, TYPICALLY BY STOCKPILING FOOD & SUPPLIES.

HEY OREGON_DAVE, MY NAME IS ANT & I SAW YOUR POSTING ABOUT YOUR NEW HOME BUNKER ON PREPPERFORUM. I LIVE IN OREGON TOO & WAS WONDERING IF I COULD COME & SEE IT IN PERSON. I WAS THINKING ABOUT BUILDING SOMETHING SIMILAR FOR MY HOME. —ANT

CAMP SUN LAKE

OREGON DAVE, IN THE LIVIN' FLESH! I WAS BEGINNING TO THINK YOU WERE SOME NSA ROBOT OR SOMETHING.

YOU MUST BE ANT.

WELP, FOLLOW ME, I'LL SHOW YOU MY BUNKER.

I REALLY APPRECIATE THIS DAVE!

LATER...

THE END.

disperse

by Lori Lubeski

disperse you

trace me, trace me trace me back
until before you,

until before there was you—

forward until the after-effects of you wear off

how I never want you to be gone from me
I want a spell put on me—

to quietly disperse you across the field
of my existence

the way my mother's ashes

From *pilgrimage foliage*

remembrances

when we were
bells
summer light
touched us
and our
voices
glimmered

Note from Management

by Gregory Lawless

Please, remember
to leave the poem
the way you found it.

Contributors

Harvey Blume is an author (*Ota Benga: The Pygmy At The Zoo*, 1992), free-lance writer and critic, who hails from the other Brooklyn, the part they haven't branded yet.

Jonathan Escoffery is the winner of the 2016 Waasnode Fiction Prize and a 2017 Somerville Arts Council Artist Fellowship. His writing has been selected to appear in *Prairie Schooner, Passages North, The Caribbean Writer, Salt Hill Journal, Solstice*, and elsewhere. Jonathan earned his MFA in Fiction from the University of Minnesota, and has taught Creative Writing at UMN and at GrubStreet in Boston.

Glynnis Fawkes is a cartoonist and archaeological illustrator living in Vermont. Her comics may be seen on Muthamagazine.com, classical-inquiries.chs.harvard.edu, and glynnisfawkes.com. Her book *Alle Ego* won the Society of Illustrators MoCCA Arts Festival Award and her comics were nominated for an Ignatz Award in 2016.

Richard Garcia's recent books *The Other Odyssey*, from Dream Horse Press, and *The Chair*, from BOA, were both published in 2015. His forthcoming book, *Porridge*, was published by Press 53 in March of 2016. His poems have appeared in many journals, including *The Georgia Review* and *Spillway*, and in anthologies such as *The Pushcart Prize* and *Best American Poetry*. He lives in Charleston, S.C. and is on the staff of the Antioch Low Residency MFA in Los Angeles.

Melissa Ginsburg is the author of the poetry collection *Dear Weather Ghost* and the noir novel *Sunset City*, April 2016. Her poems have appeared in *Fence, Denver Quarterly, Copper Nickel, Blackbird*, and other magazines. She has received support for her work from the Ucross Foundation and the Mississippi Arts Council. She teaches creative writing and literature at the University of Mississippi in Oxford.

Katie Green is a journalist, writer, and filmmaker. She attended the Ma'aleh Film School of Jerusalem where both her graduate films "Prague" and "16" were shown on Israel's Channel 2. She is Festivals Coordinator at the Ma'aleh Film School and an independent editor and translator, with a specialty in subtitling films. Her stories and poetry have appeared in

Jewishfiction.net, *Cyclamens and Swords*, and *Yew Journal*. In 2015 her story "The Color of Sand" was short-listed for the Moment Short Story Fiction prize.

Jennifer Haigh lives in Boston. Her short fiction has been published in *Granta, Electric Literature, The Best American Short Stories*, and many other places. Her fifth novel, *Heat and Light*, was published this year by Ecco. Find her at www.jennifer-haigh.com

Merissa Khurma is a Senior Policy Advisor at the Boston Consortium for Arab Region Studies (BCARS) and a 2016 Harvard Mason Fellow. She has worked in international relations and security analysis, diplomacy, gender development, fiscal reform, workforce development, and the Syrian refugee crisis. Merissa served as Director of the Office of HRH Prince Ali Bin Al Hussein and as Press Attache and Director of the Jordan Information Bureau at the Embassy in Washington, DC.

Nick Lantz is the author of four books of poetry, most recently *You, Beast* (University of Wisconsin Press, 2017). He teaches in the MFA program at Sam Houston State University and lives in Huntsville, Texas.

Gregory Lawless is the author of, most recently, *Far Away* (Red Mountain Press, 2015) and *Dreamburgh, Pennsylvania* (Dream Horse Press, forthcoming).

Lori Lubeski is the author of *Dissuasion Crowds the Slow Worker; STAMINA; Obedient, A body; eyes dipped in longitude lines;* and *Undermined*. She collaborated with printmaker Jakub Kalousek on *TRICKLE* and *Sweet Land,* and with artist Jeannette Landrie on *has the river of the body risen*. New work is featured in *Let The Bucket Down*, and her forthcoming poetry collection, *pilgrimage foliage*, will be published this year by Spot Lit Press. Lori lives in Boston, where she teaches at Curry College and Boston University.

Timothy Patrick McCarthy is an award-winning scholar, educator, and activist. He holds a joint faculty appointment in Harvard's undergraduate honors program in History and Literature, the Graduate School of Education, and the John F. Kennedy School of Government, where he is Core Faculty and Director of Culture Change & Social Justice Initiatives at the Carr Center for Human Rights Policy. Educated at Harvard and Columbia, Dr. McCarthy is the author or editor of five books from the New Press, including *Stonewall's Children: Living Queer History in the Age of Liberation,*

Loss, and Love. His essay "Coming of AIDS" was published in *Pangyrus* in January 2015. "Provincetown Sketches" is the first installment in a series of creative non-fiction pieces about contemporary queer life in Province-town, Massachusetts.

Carrie Oeding's first book of poems, *Our List of Solutions*, is from 42 Miles Press. Her work has appeared in *The Awl, Denver Quarterly, Pleiades, Columbia Poetry Review,* and elsewhere.

Jennifer Perrine is the author of *No Confession, No Mass,* winner of the 2014 Prairie Schooner Book Prize in Poetry; *In the Human Zoo,* recipient of the 2010 Agha Shahid Ali Poetry Prize; and *The Body Is No Machine,* winner of the 2008 Devil's Kitchen Reading Award in Poetry. For more information, visit www.jenniferperrine.org

Carroll Sandel's work has appeared in *Hippocampus Magazine, The Drum,* and *Grub Daily.* She was a 2014 finalist for the Dorothy Cappon non-fiction prize in New Letters, and has recently completed a memoir, *Lying Eyes,* which explores her untrustworthy memories and how certainty about our memories can betray us.

Julie Wittes Schlack won a Hopwood Award for Fiction and was a finalist for the Annie Dillard Creative Nonfiction award, the A Room of Her Own Foundation's Clarissa Dalloway award, and for the Glimmer Train Fiction prize. She wrote book reviews for the *Boston Globe,* and is a regular contributor to *Cognoscenti.* Her work has appeared or is forthcoming in numerous journals, including *Shenandoah, The Writer's Chronicle, The Louisville Review, Phoebe, Sanskrit, South Carolina Review, Ninth Letter, Saint Ann's Review, Eleven Eleven,* and *Tampa Review.* Julie lives with her husband in the Boston area and is a graduate of Lesley University's low-residency MFA program in Creative Writing.

J. Arthur Scott is a writer living in Brooklyn.

Maggie Smith is the author of *Weep Up* (Tupelo Press, forthcoming 2018); *The Well Speaks of Its Own Poison* (Tupelo Press 2015), winner of the Dorset Prize and the 2016 Independent Publisher Book Awards Gold Medal in Poetry; *Lamp of the Body* (Red Hen 2005), winner of the Benjamin Saltman Award; and three prizewinning chapbooks. Her poems have appeared in *The Paris Review, The Southern Review, Magma, Waxwing, Virginia Quarterly Review, Guernica,* and many other journals. The recipient of fellowships from the National Endowment for the Arts, the Ohio Arts Council, and the Sustainable Arts Foundation, Smith is a freelance writer and editor, and serves as a consulting editor to the *Kenyon Review*.

Enzo Silon Surin is a Haitian-born poet, publisher, advocate, and author of the chapbook *Higher Ground* (Finishing Line Press). He was the 2015 PEN New England Celebrated New Voice in Poetry, and his most recent poems can be found in *Jubilat, Soundings East,* and *The BreakBeat Poets* anthology, among others.

Jon Thompson teaches twentieth-century/contemporary literature at North Carolina State University. His recent books are *The Book of the Floating World, After Paradise,* and *Landscape with Light.* In 2016, Shearsman Books published his latest collection of poems, *Strange Country.* He edits the international online journal, *Free Verse: A Journal of Contemporary Poetry & Poetics* and the poetry series, *Free Verse Editions.* More on him can be found at www.jon-thompson.net

Rodrigo Toscano's newest book of poetry, *Explosion Rocks Springfield,* came out from Fence Books in spring 2016. *Collapsible Poetics Theater* was a National Poetry Series selection. His poetry has appeared in the anthologies *Angels of the Americlypse, Voices Without Borders, Diasporic Avant Gardes, Imagined Theatres, In the Criminal's Cabinet,* and *Best American Poetry.* He works for the Labor Institute based in NYC. He now lives in the Faubourg Marigny (seventh ward) of New Orleans.

Aaron Whitaker is a cartoonist and screenwriter who lives in Los Angeles, California. He is the author of several comics including *Globes, Bangs & Beard Diary, The Awkward Quarterly,* and the graphic novel *The City Troll.*

Anton Yakovlev studied filmmaking and poetry at Harvard University. He is the author of poetry chapbooks *Ordinary Impalers* (Aldrich Press, 2017), *The Ghost of Grant Wood* (Finishing Line Press, 2015), and *Neptune Court* (The Operating System, 2015). His poems have appeared in *The New Yorker, The Hopkins Review, Prelude, Measure, The Stockholm Review of Literature,* and elsewhere. *The Last Poet of the Village,* a book of translations of poetry by Sergei Esenin, is forthcoming from Sensitive Skin Books in 2017. He has also written and directed several short films.

Zabel Yessayan emerged into the tumultuous, multiethnic world of late 19th-century Constantinople at a time when Sultan Abdul Hamid unleashed his fury on both Christian minorities and the progressive elements of Ottoman society. Yessayan crossed ethnic and religious boundaries and fought for human rights while the world collapsed around her. Her work has been translated into English by the Zabel Yessayan Project, which has generously allowed *Pangyrus* to republish the pieces found in this edition.

ABOUT PANGYRUS

Pangyrus is a Boston-based group of writers, editors, and artists with a new vision for how high-quality creative work can prosper online and in print. We aim to foster a community of individuals and organizations dedicated to art, ideas, and making culture thrive.

Combining Pangaea and gyrus, the terms for the world continent and whorls of the cerebral cortex crucial to verbal association, Pangyrus is about connection.

INDEX by AUTHOR and GENRE

CPSIA information can be obtained
at www.ICGtesting.com
Printed in the USA
BVOW09s0454030817
490947BV00001B/7/P